I0640118

Amsterdam in Ultramarine

A R Grogan

Published by Andrew Grogan, 2025.

This is a work of fiction. Similarities to real people, places, or events are entirely coincidental.

AMSTERDAM IN ULTRAMARINE

First edition. April 6, 2025.

Copyright © 2025 A R Grogan.

ISBN: 978-0991159260

Written by A R Grogan.

Amsterdam in Ultramarine

By Andy Grogan

I'm a British writer who spent twenty-five years living in Amsterdam—a city that never stopped surprising me. I fell in love with its canals and crooked houses, its stubborn beauty, its deep contradictions. It's a place that feels small but contains worlds; a city that is both grounded and ethereal, practical and visionary, deeply tolerant yet fiercely private. Living there shaped the way I see history, culture, power—and time.

Now based in New York, I'm struck by the echoes of Amsterdam that still ripple through this city: in its design, in its ideals, and in the bones of modern capitalism. What began in the merchant houses along the Herengracht resonates in the skyscrapers of Manhattan. Amsterdam's influence on global finance, trade, and thought is not just historical—it's foundational.

Amsterdam in Ultramarine is, at heart, a love letter to that city. It's also a meditation on time, memory, privilege, and legacy. Through the lens of a mystery thriller—laced with elements of speculative fiction and historical intrigue—I've tried to capture something essential about Amsterdam: that its past is always present, and its stories are never truly over.

This is a city that remembers.

Andy Grogan

Photographs Andy Grogan
Copyright Text Andy Grogan 2025
Sketch and Oil painting Rembrandt Van Rijn

A Love Letter to Amsterdam

Chapter 1

In a whirlwind of disorientation and terror, I was plummeting from a bridge at the tip of Manhattan toward Manhattan's East River's cold embrace. Someone had thrown me off like a piece of trash. My hands first frantically grasped for anything within reach, only to find empty air slipping through my fingers. The starlight above mingled with the bridge's glaring lights mirrored in the murky depths below. Terror clouded my senses—where did the sky end and the river begin?

As I fell, time seemed to stretch, each heartbeat echoing in my ears like a countdown to oblivion. The city overshadowed, indifferent to my plight, its vibrant life continuing as if I were just another fleeting shadow. I braced myself for impact, the cold water promising a chilling embrace that felt both terrifying and inevitable. At that moment, I resolved to fight against the fate that awaited me beneath the surface.

But then, an eerie serenity permeated me. With my muscles tense and my breath held tight, instinct took control, causing my legs to align and my feet to tilt downward, breaking the surface of the water. Many thoughts flashed through my head, but I only had one thought as I hit the water, still unsure if I would survive.

Revenge.

My body collided forcefully with the water, buckling my knees upon impact. I felt the rapid deceleration reverberate through my core.

Instantly, an icy chill enveloped me, the balmy New York night air cooled by the confluence of cold Atlantic seawater and freshwater from the Hudson River. The act's brutality took me by surprise. This was not what I had expected of the Van Os family. But this was the proof I wasn't merely a paranoid soul lost in a conspiracy; I was seeking the truth about a secret society.

I had been investigating insider trading for several years, spanning multiple years and at least two continents. It involved the secret mega-rich. Their wealth and secrecy led to speculation about their existence. They did not appear on the Forbes list of billionaires. There was a firewall of greed that they hid behind.

The breakthrough began a few weeks earlier in Amsterdam, where I live. Amsterdam is a city beloved by many for its beauty and significance. Like Jerusalem, New York, or Paris, it holds a special place in the hearts of those who have lived there. This is not just any typical European city. Perhaps because of its relatively small size, people often underestimate Amsterdam's historical significance. It is renowned for its long history of freedom and independence. Stepping onto its cobblestone streets and taking in the canals and narrow houses transports you to a different era, brimming with possibility and promise. The birthplace of liberal freedom. It truly is a gem among cities.

I love Amsterdam; it is my cherished city. It is a vibrant and bustling metropolis, with bicycles zooming by on winding streets and beautiful canals lined with colorful houses and flower boxes. The architecture varies from modern structures to centuries-old buildings, all coexisting in a style of tolerance. The air is fragrant with the delightful scents of freshly baked stroopwafels and brewing coffee. Cannabis scents drift by occasionally, enhancing Amsterdam's eclectic mix of aromas. This is more than just a tourist destination; it is a living city. It is a place where families raise their children, students pursue their dreams, and visitors from all walks of life come to experience its magic.

A stack of prints containing historical records from the archives in Albany, New York, was just placed on my desk at the main police station on the Marnixstraat. These were for my pet project. For a few years, I had been quietly nurturing this investigation, barely tolerated by my superior. I was certain that somewhere within these documents lay the key to proving my theory about organized crime in the dark shadow world of finance in the Dutch capital. I had a personal agenda, a score to settle. But I needed proof. Everything till now was conjecture. I was getting close. Little did I know, but being thrown from a bridge would show me how close I was.

Rumors circulated around the police station about the discovery of another shriveled corpse, but I deliberately chose not to become involved in that case. It would only distract me from my mission. The historical documents would keep me occupied for some time. But then, from across the busy floor, Captain de Burg yelled for me to come to his office. It was clear he wasn't pleased, and I already knew why. I had messed up once again.

'Sit down, Dol!' he yelled at me in Dutch. We had to enact a situation akin to a master and servant dynamic. His usual frustration with me led him to assert his dominance before the team, so I feigned repentance. I gestured towards the door to suggest that I should keep it open so the on-duty police officers on the floor could clearly hear him scolding me. We had an understanding. He nodded yes, then pointed at the chair in front of his desk. He was very Dutch. Heavy from the Edam cheese, beer, and boerenkool met worst. His hair, thin and blond, was crew cut to conceal his impending hair loss. He is tall, just like everyone else here.

'What the hell were you thinking? Why did you turn up at an arrest team assignment in a limo wearing a tuxedo? Who were you trying to impress? Is this supposed to be professional? Were you trying to be funny?' He yelled at the door.

This had indeed happened; although I did not intend to make such an irreverent appearance, a combination of unfortunate logistics, flight delays, and a party at my brother's investment bank was more enjoyable than I thought it would be. It was a fancy-dress party, and I went as Gatsby. I wore a fake mustache. That's all there is to that story. I should have called in sick, but that's not how my parents raised me.

I apologized loudly and profusely toward the door and said I had screwed up (although I omitted to say the word "again") and made promises about improvement, and the captain yelled more at the door; as usual, he wanted the last word. The captain barked about team discipline, loyalty, and resources.

Of course, I had made mistakes in the past. For example, my Japanese personal manservant and bodyguard insisted on bringing me his self-made sushi for lunch daily. I had to intervene with Hiro, and my office space was now off-limits.

So let me freeze-frame the captain in mid-rant—mouth open, a piece of spittle launching mid-air, a vein on his temple in mid-throb, slightly cross-eyed, one eyelid half-closed, face distorted like a pause on a video call. Let's talk about something more interesting; let's talk about ME!

My name is Boudewijna Dol, the daughter of Boudewijn and Pascal Dol. So yes, let's get that out of the way. There are two important things you should know about the Dol family. First, Dol, in Dutch, means crazy or passionate, or love. But in Holland, weird names are the norm. Freek is a common boy's name, as is Vaart, a common last name. The Dutch used a patronymic system where the father's first name became the first son's last name. The other kids got the leftover names from their grandfather, great-grandfather, and so on.

The tradition in my family, which dates back to the 1600s, was to name the firstborn son Boudewijn. However, the whole birth experience so horrified my mother that she declared me not only the first but definitely the last, renaming me Boudewijn-a. Ironically, a year later, she became pregnant again, this time with twins. I now have a younger brother and a sister. She called them Theo and Thea, which was again very unfortunate, as a year or two later, a comedy duo became famous in Holland, called Theo and Thea. We are not lucky with names—the Dol family.

However, we are fortunate in other aspects of our lives. The second thing you should know about the Dol family is that we are extremely wealthy. I wonder why they describe money negatively—they are stinking, disgustingly, obscenely rich.

Well, we are wealthy. This needs some explanation. There is "rich," and there is "wealthy." Being wealthy implies that your wealth is sustainable, whereas being rich implies that if you are a fool, you could end up impoverished at some point. This often happens with the rich but never the wealthy.

So, where did this wealth come from? One of my ancestors set up the Dol Cookie Factory. "Dol op Dol Cookies!" was the rather obvious sales pitch. This made my ancestor (yes, you guessed it, Boudewijn Dol) a rich man.

Now, high-energy, entrepreneurial alpha males with money don't idle away their time baking cookies. So, he branched out into other "activities." The next endeavor was paling, an eel-like fish popular in Holland today.

A warning to myself. As a historian, I have a tendency to stray from the principal topic of historical stories, so I try to keep my historical side notes to only one paragraph. Boudewijn Dol entered the paling business. His paling was from the North Sea and was of exceptional quality. The meat was more succulent and lasted longer in brine, something to do with a gland in the intestines. To show the difference between his better product and the inferior paling from elsewhere, he branded (brand means to burn in Dutch) the wooden vats with his trademark—Dol op Hollandsche Paling. That was his brand, and that's where the term "brand" originated.

Boudewijn Dol, having recognized the value of a brand, ventured into a variety of high-quality products, ranging from Indonesian coffee, cocoa, and spices to German machine parts and American oil. By the 1900s, the Dol family had become not just rich, but exceptionally wealthy. Being Dutch at the core, we Dols are comparatively frugal, and our diverse investments grew exponentially faster than we could ever spend. We bought Apple, Amazon, and Google. At the start.

Was my family involved in insider trading? This was a crucial question I posed to myself. As a family member, I would have an advantage in discovering the financial secrets of my ancestors. I was unsuccessful in uncovering any information. They had been fortunate enough to hold on to their shares when others were selling. But that was always their modus operandi. They had also invested in some bad opportunities. Their financial picture appeared to be fairly honest. They were as honest as any extremely wealthy family could be.

Despite growing up in such an affluent environment, I encountered families who were significantly wealthier than ours. They had been so wealthy for such a long time that they appeared to exist in a different world and era. They seemed detached from the ordinary world we all inhabit. I could discern this from the clothing they donned. The perfume. The accent was something you could never quite place. They employed phrases such as "sanguine," "thither," and "on the morrow." And when you visited one of their stately homes, there were so many rooms. Often, you could enter a room to find its furniture covered in sheets, undisturbed for years. As if they had all gone to bed. Like some sort of museum. It doesn't matter how rich you are; you can only be in one room at a time and swim in one pool at a time. They simply had too much.

You may wonder, why am I working at a police station in Amsterdam, enduring this grief and abuse from my captain? Good question. Self-knowledge is a wonderful thing. I am a spoiled, entitled rich kid who is pathologically incapable of doing something that doesn't interest me. It's hard to have discipline when there are no consequences if you don't do what you don't want to do. Because of this, the stress of depending solely on my income is something I've never experienced. I don't worry about squandering money as a resource. I don't worry about failure in material pursuits or about not experiencing amazing things and meeting incredible people. Such wonders are as accessible to me as breath itself.

It's not my fault; I wish everyone could have this. It was thrust upon me; I didn't ask for it. I am not complaining, either; that would be ungrateful! I went through a dark guilt period as a teenager, but I learned how to embrace my circumstances thanks to expensive therapy (oh, the irony). I am worldly and experienced in many things, but naïve in other areas.

Unlike my rich kid friends from the international ski slopes, my parents raised us with Dutch *nuchterheid*. Our parents kept our clogs firmly planted in the fertile, muddy polder soil of the lowlands. I had to clean my bedroom before the maids arrived. I had to bring my plates to the kitchen for the staff. Maria required me to place my dirty clothes in the laundry basket for her to wash and fold. Well, you get the picture.

I am accustomed to following my path. But I am fortunate that, despite my permanently intense, distracted, and kaleidoscopic childhood, I have found focus on one thing. My passion is history. It is my rock, friend, religion, framework, and sometimes, my nemesis. I studied European history at Oxford and Paris and got my Ph.D. in European economic history in Amsterdam.

It is exceedingly geeky, but there is a rationale for my employment at the Amsterdam Police Station on the Marnixstraat. The Dol family established generous trust funds for their descendants, but these funds come with specific conditions. There are two branches. You can become a Dol employee and apprentice through the Dol family enterprise. Starting at the lowest level, the Dol family enterprise rotates you through various functions to evaluate your successes and failures. Eventually, the Dol family enterprise finds a suitable fit. Most of my cousins and nieces have traveled this path and have found it fair and rewarding.

Alternatively, if you opt to remain outside the firm, as I did, you will receive a trust fund that is less substantial but still quite generous. There is one catch. The recipient of this generosity must be involved in meaningful employment. A niece of mine works for an environmental agency; another does pro-bono legal work. I am a detective at the Korps Nationale Politie in Amsterdam. They provide you with sufficient resources to accomplish tasks, but they do not provide any resources for idle activities.

Agreed, I rarely hear the faint plop of my salary as it drips in my ocean of a bank account, but it guarantees my membership in the trust fund club. The rest of the family refers to us as "the civilians" and smile indulgently at us.

And yes, the observant reader will wonder if we have a family member who does not fit into these categories. Indeed, as in all families, we have our black sheep. Perhaps I will elaborate on my cherished cousin Vincent in the future.

I possess the attractive looks of my French mother, but unfortunately, living among the tall Dutch, I also have her petite frame. I am in my middle thirties and can shoot a gun (thanks to my training in the police corps).

Anyway, since it's been a while, I'm going to unfreeze our friend, Captain de Burg, and allow him to continue his rant. I allowed him to yell at the door while I caught up on some texts on my phone. Meanwhile, he paced around his office, occasionally slamming his fat hand on his desk for dramatic effect. Eventually, he went over to the door and closed it. The theater piece for the other officers on the duty floor was now over.

'We have another one,' he said quietly. 'We found it in a car at Schiphol.' I put away my smartphone and paid attention. 'Show me,' I said. I didn't want to be interested, but I can't help myself. The old, stuffy documents from Albany will have to wait.

'First, no more nonsense with tuxedos and limos. You must play by the rules if you want to remain employed here and enjoy the force's privileges. There are no entitlements here. You know this, and that limo was an own goal. You're smarter than that.'

I nodded. That incident did not reflect well on me. Favoritism and privilege were detrimental to the team's morale, and the captain needed to maintain a tight ship with disciplined officers. Privilege and favoritism are unacceptable in Dutch culture. I had already reached the position of detective in a way that appeared to be expedited for some. Which it probably was. I wasn't the most popular officer on the team, and I wasn't completely blameless. Those of us who are wealthy often have poor interpersonal skills.

When the Amsterdam Police rescued the beer magnate Freddie Heineken from his kidnappers, he wanted to reward them with better equipment, but they disallowed it because it might encourage favoritism for the wealthy. The Dutch sometimes overthink things, but that's the culture, and I must work within it.

I could resign and continue working as a specialist contractor, but there were disadvantages. My authority as a badged detective provided me with invaluable access to doors and archives. My contacts with the ultra-wealthy were a tremendous asset to the force. Also, I unostentatiously funded my own investigations. No expense claims ever went to accounting on my watch. Captain der Burg made flagrant misuse of that and sent me cases that kept me interested and his budget healthy. We adhered to the famous Dutch policy of mutual tolerance. That's why he was giving me the mummified corpse case. No motives, no murder weapons, no actual cause of death except old age. It was barely a case, but it still needed attention.

'Show me,' I said again, hands outstretched, fingers wiggling like a child grasping candy. He frowned, grabbed a folder from his desk, and handed me the file. I opened it up. There were photos of a high-range car, a Jaguar, with a dead body in the driving seat. Someone had parked the car in Schiphol Airport's "Premium first-class" car park. The car had tinted windows, and it had remained there for about a week before anyone investigated. The body, dressed in a modern, high-quality Armani suit, appeared mummified as if it had been dead for centuries. It looked like some student joke. This was the fourth one in three weeks.

The captain snatched the file back. 'Again, keep this quiet. Pick a small team for this one; I'm tired of you going solo. Volunteers only.' I nodded, and he reluctantly handed back the file for me to study.

I walk back to my desk, deep in thought, engrossed in the file. One of the other agents slaps me on the back, 'So Buffy, got yourself ripped a new one again, huh?'

Hilarious. An intriguing factoid is that the agent who referred to me as Buffy is Jaap van de Geintje. Now, the term "geintje" not only refers to a small brook or stream, but it also connotes a joke, which he frequently tells. Constantly.

Overall, my colleagues are good people. One colleague shows more curiosity about me than my work, a trait I dislike. Another colleague is envious of everyone around him. To avoid his obsessive ambitions, I steer clear of him. Apart from that, they're a decent bunch. Now, I need to choose a team.

No, wait. Let's dig deeper into the details before I recruit. There were four corpses found to date. So, what were the other three?

They found the first victim in a ditch hidden among the sprawling trees of Amsterdam Woods. He sat atop a luxurious e-bike, now mummified and preserved in its last moments. The tracks revealed an eerily peaceful scene—it appeared he had been enjoying a leisurely ride before meeting his untimely demise. But how did he end up in the ditch? It wasn't particularly deep, only reaching up to his knees. If it were Halloween, his lifeless body would blend in perfectly with the eerie surroundings. Yet, even in death, there was a sense of irony to his posture—frozen in a grimace that appeared more like laughter at the fish swimming below. Such a strange and tragic sight amidst the natural beauty of the woods.

We found Number Two dead in a prostitute's window in the red-light district. I lead the discovery team. The rooms were tiny and claustrophobic, and the blue UV lights of our forensic team contrasted with the red lights of the street. The corpse had the same petrified mummy state—the same grimace.

It looks like a happy ending to me, said van der Geintje. We had all crowded into the small room—eight agents, mostly 6 foot five, and me, a full foot and three inches shorter. Even my uniform was a half size too big; it made me look like a child playing cops and robbers. The victim had been a client and had asked the girl for a glass of water. When she came back, he was dead, and it looked like he had been dead for hundreds of years. The sheets' lack of staining at the contact points struck me as strange. He appeared perfectly desiccated, as though someone had freeze-dried the fluids and life force from him.

'He looks dehydrated,' I said dryly—I can joke, too. They started chuckling. 'Maybe if we throw a bucket of water over him, he will come back to life,' someone added. We all giggled but then attempted to suppress our laughter. This was serious business, but that made it harder to stop laughing. So, we broke up the group—thank god, it was getting really stuffy—and we let forensics do their job. I interviewed the "hostess." She was distraught, and I could not get much out of her.

'He was well-paid and desired the full treatment. He paid more than requested. He had good manners, but he seemed nervous. He said, 'Might as well enjoy myself while it lasts.' I don't know what you're thinking, but I didn't do that to him.'

Number three was sitting on a tram. He boarded the tram, took a seat, and soon after, a fellow passenger noticed that something was wrong. Ironically, it was Tram 7 that passed our headquarters on the Marnixstraat. Again, he was mummified. There was some blurry CCTV footage from the tram. He was sitting there, obsessively checking his cell phone. It was difficult to see him; he was wearing a hoodie and sunglasses as if trying to remain incognito. Then, at one point, his head leans and rests on the window, and he stops checking his phone—a quiet, peaceful, painless death.

So now I had two piles of folders on my desk. My original case with the historical prints from Albany and this new petrified mummy case. I knew the captain wanted me to prioritize the mummies, so I reluctantly pushed Albany aside and started work. I was looking for patterns and coincidences.

They were all male, and based on their identification documents, their estimated age was approximately eighty years. The first commonality I discovered was their registration at the Amsterdam civil registry, known as the bevolkingsregister. Later, their parents claimed that the Dutch resistance had destroyed their birth details through arson during the Second World War. After the war, the same civil servant re-registered all four victims within a week of each other. Suspicious.

The hooker had not mentioned that he was eighty years old, so I would have to check on that. The forensics had not come back with more details yet. Apparently, they were all successful businessmen, not directly related, either through family or business. They were often abroad, but each had an apartment in Amsterdam. There were photos of family and children in their wallets. The smartphones had high-end encryption.

The desk sergeant called and said I had a visitor. She had time-sensitive information about the 'mummies.' I thought it might be the hooker, so I asked the desk sergeant to send her to my desk. It was not the hooker, but a petite-looking woman with a Mediterranean complexion. She seemed about forty and was well-dressed. She introduced herself as the sister of the man we had found in the car at Schiphol Airport.

'My name is Fernandina Peres,' she said in English. She apologized; her Dutch was not what it used to be. I told her that my Dutch had improved, but I considered English my mother language, although my Spanish and Italian were passable. I provided her with a few examples, but I realized I should have been questioning her, not making it about myself. I do that. I'm told it's adorable. I asked her to sit, but she insisted on going to a private room. I agreed, so we proceeded to one of the empty interrogation rooms.

She said she lived together with her brother, or at least when he was in Spain, which was about six months a year. He had his own consultancy business, helping companies trade between EU and non-EU countries, often with companies in New York.

She was pretty and elegant and seemed cultured. She was well-groomed, her long black hair carefully plaited in a style reminiscent of Spain.

'He was an amiable man, very sophisticated. Very elegant. Despite his marriage, he never had children. His wife was dead. He was in Amsterdam for business and to go to the wedding.'

She pulls out a letter from her Vuitton handbag. I request permission to read the handwritten letter. She nods, but I tell her she must agree verbally, and she does. The letter is written to her by Miguel; it is rambling and references things I would need more clarification on. Then he writes that his time is ending soon, that this thing he had feared was approaching. He said it had already started to happen, and there was no stopping it. I ask her for clarification.

'Miguel told me he was part of a secret society. The group, belonging to an elite family, regarded themselves as superior to mortal humans. He claimed he inherited this trait from his parents. He said that he had superior powers of longevity and strength. This explains why he did not age as quickly as other people. He informed me he was significantly older than I initially believed and that his powers would soon diminish, ultimately leading to his death. I don't understand how this could all come true.'

She began to cry and reached for a tissue, so I went to grab her a glass of water. I got some coffee, tea, and cookies from the canteen. I ensured the video and audio were working and asked Maria, a victim specialist, to join us. Upon my return, I was so shocked that the tray of cookies and coffee went flying. Maria screamed. Fernandina was mummified. I was mortified.

The other agents arrived quickly and surveyed the scene. Rarely did the Corps' Politie headquarters become a crime scene. We processed everything we could. We scrutinized her belongings, which appeared to confirm the information she had been providing. The video showed her, after I left, grasping the bag to her chest as if in pain but then relaxing, her head downward; she seemed to contract, like an inflated doll, leaking her life force out into the cold interrogation room. It seemed such a juxtaposition—this once-elegant lady and the sterile, cement-walled, neon-lit room.

'I was just talking to her.' I said.

'I know you can be boring sometimes, Buffy, but...' said van der Geintje.

'Not now, Jaap,' I said. He was not good at feeling the room. The captain came in, looked at what was happening, and then told me, 'My office, now!'

I followed him to the office, holding up my pants with one hand as they kept slipping down. I was going to get them tailored, but I never seem to have time. Not great optics: even my gun holster belt had once slipped around my ankles during a staff presentation. I should remember to text Hiro. He would know what to do.

I sat in the same chair I had sat in that morning when the captain had berated me for my tuxedo escapade. Now I had some more explaining to do.

'Report,' he said. His arms crossed, waiting for my best effort.

'The theory about the mummies was that it was some student joke, but the red-light district mummy, and now this recent case, has shown that there must be a different explanation. I am collaborating with forensics to explore the potential connection between them and the rare medical condition that may have affected them. Other leads suggest they're distantly related. Another lead is that they were all in Amsterdam for a wedding. This remains unconfirmed.'

This was not entirely true, but I had not much to go on. Actually, Fernandina's statement—that he was going to "the" wedding, not "a" wedding—was the sole basis for this. It's a stretch.

I proceeded: 'They appear to have business ties to global corporations, with a preference for New York.' They are wealthy; they have socio-economic ties and business connections to the Netherlands, and especially Amsterdam. They were all born here. Until now, all of them have been male, which is a statistical anomaly. I believe there could be similarities between these cases and the larger Van Os cases I've been working on.

The captain groaned; he thought my pet project about links to the underworld of dark finance in Amsterdam and New York was a little strained and out of our remit. These were the historical files from Albany I still needed to study. His job was to keep the streets of Amsterdam safe for the local inhabitants and the tourists. Everything else was simply the result of foolish, wealthy individuals exploiting one another, and it was not of any concern to him. I doubt he even had a trust fund. I knew my project was not a priority for him. He had made that clear.

'First, Dol, don't go down any rabbit holes looking for dark finance or supernatural phenomena. I want you to show me you can chase the facts and keep a level head. I know about these silly rumors of vampires and zombies, but that's a distraction.'

So, let me be clear: I was totally on board about avoiding the supernatural nonsense. I had not started the rumors, and it was in my best interest to quash my vampire-slayer reputation. My instincts warned me that this was fanciful fake news or, more likely, a deceptive scheme. People were trying to create confusion and false leads in order to hide the true story.

Get me the facts. "What are your next steps?" he inquired.

'I'm going to crash a wedding.'

Chapter 2

So, believe me on this one: you don't get to be a trust-fund brat and not have a lot of connections with the party scene, especially in Amsterdam. Once I was back at my desk, I quickly reached out to a few friends to inquire about any planned significant weddings in Amsterdam. Sarah delivered the goods. There was a private wedding in the Nieuwe Kerk (that's where the Kings and Queens get married, by the way). She said it was super private. Sarah struggled to secure an invitation, a situation that was highly unusual for her.

After a few phone calls (a friend of the mayor of Amsterdam got me the tickets; she owes me); I was added to the wedding list. The wedding was on Friday. I wondered whether this was the wedding Ms. Perez mentioned or if the other victims were supposed to attend. But it was the Van Os family, the very clan I had been investigating, and until forensics returned with more information or at least other leads, I didn't want any trails to go cold.

The Nieuwe Kerk stands in the center of Amsterdam, its Gothic architecture and intricate carvings drawing the eye. Its spire reaches towards the clouds, a symbol of strength and stability. The bustling square is a mix of tourists and locals, their movements a blur against the stunning backdrop of the church. It stands next to the Royal Palace on the Dam, the heart of Amsterdam.

The ground beneath me is a mix of rough cobblestones and smooth pavement, worn down by the constant foot traffic. As I walk, I can feel the slight vibration of trams and the whoosh of bikes passing by.

I took my place in the church, sitting at the back, trying to be as anonymous as possible. I recognized several individuals from the wealthy tribes. There were Janzen-Tels. They became wealthy when they created a mechanism that transformed the turning motion of Dutch windmills into the sawing motion of a wood-cutting blade, making wood production cheaper. They diversified their accumulated riches into other areas, transforming them into wealth over the centuries.

Then there were the Ganzenvelds. They had taken advantage of the new low-cost wood production and built boats that could sail to the Dogger Bank in the North Sea, where they fished the tasty paling. These new large boats could house a crew working on the paling as the ship sailed back to Amsterdam. The crew had neatly filleted the eels and placed them in brine vats before the ship docked. Over there were the Truerniets. They were New Money, something to do with antidepressants.

The first rows of seats were still empty. Then the guests arrived from a side entrance. The expensive black SUVs with dark-tinted windows deposited the family members like a conveyor belt, while the betrothed families entered the church. Strangely, given the beautiful weather, a black canopy stood at the entrance. They sat down. Big floppy hats and dark sunglasses. Roughly ten bodyguards, dressed in suits and wearing earpieces, assumed strategic positions around the church. The ceremony went well; the bride was lovely and giggly and seemed very young, while the groom looked nervous and unseasonably pale.

I swiped a wedding list from one attendant. All the usual suspects in the big families in Amsterdam were in attendance. The groom's family, the Van Os, became wealthy in the 1600s when they established the VOC, the Vereenigde Oostindische Compagnie, which laid the foundation for modern capitalism. Their name dispersed into many global interests over the years, and they went dark after the kidnapping of Heineken, the beer magnate, and the kidnapping and murder of Geert-Jan Heijn (of the Albert Heijn stores) in the 1980s. I tried to take some photos with my phone, but a security guard stopped me (in a vulgar way, I might add) and made me delete the images. Luckily, everything I take goes straight to the cloud. So there.

The ceremony concluded with an announcement of a reception at the Amstel Hotel, followed by a canal boat ride to Pampus, an island in the Ijmeer, for pampering.

I cycled to my flat on the Herengracht and changed into my party outfit. Hiro had laid it out on my bed, along with a snack in the kitchen and the right accessories. Hiro is amazing, and strangely enough, I hardly ever see him. He occasionally scares the bejabbers out of me when I stumble in on him doing his thing, but besides that, he is my ninja. I picked something else to wear for the party; Hiro doesn't always get it right, then cycled down the Herengracht to the Amstel.

Amsterdam is beautiful in the spring. It is timeless. There is something magical about cycling over the small bridges, like a small boat cresting the waves of history as I pass the canal houses. Every facade tells a unique tale of merchants, traders, painters, writers, and philosophers.

There lived John Adams, the ambassador of the newly minted United States, grateful to the Netherlands for being one of the first to acknowledge its formation. Overzealous police, unaware of his identity, arrested Czar Peter of Russia for being drunk.

I dodged the tourists as I cycled along the canal. I pretended that the tourist was Erasmus, who was walking down the middle of the road. Rembrandt, always late, was hurrying to discuss a commission for a portrait. Spinoza, not paying attention, argues with his rabbi. I nearly knock a book out of the hands of an engrossed John Locke.

I make a right turn onto the Amstel, heading straight towards the hotel. The crowd at the Amstel Hotel was larger, and security was laxer. Staff kept the named families separate and guided them to the ballroom, while they treated other guests to drinks outside in a tent before transporting them on a fleet of boats. They looked a lot rougher than I had expected and soon found out why. Most were all young foreign tourists, primarily from Germany and Britain, often referred to as "Euro-trash." They all had the same story. They had been partying in the Amsterdam nightlife when some creepy guys asked if they would like to go to a big party. Free drinks and drugs. Those that were up for it had to fill in a form about where they were from and if they had any illnesses or health issues. If they passed muster, they got a text message about the location of the party. I thought it was strange. They were being vetted and sorted. As if they were looking for healthy drifters.

We sailed on the canal boats to Pampus. Techno music blared away, and the party was in full blast. In the past, sail ships arriving in Amsterdam from the far east often had to moor at Pampus, a sandbank in the Ijmeer, as they awaited a spot at the bustling Amsterdam port.

The rich flavors of exotic spices and goods from the Far East must have blended with the lingering taste of sea salt in the air. This was often an opportunity for the authorities to inspect whether there were any contagious diseases on board. While they waited, traders and loose women would come aboard and "pamper" the guests with their products and services.

Now it is a redundant fort, built on an artificial island once designed to protect Amsterdam from invasion.

The island fort, with its imposing stone buttress and hidden rooms and chambers, is the ideal place to host a goth-themed party. Given the case I was investigating, three Dracula's and a zombie on the boat were disconcerting. However, they are friendly enough and offer everyone a glass of champagne. I am allergic to alcohol and avoid anything intoxicating. Given that I am currently on duty, I took extra precautions.

The music was techno and rock. Not my scene totally; I'm more of a jazz R&B type of gal. But for dancing, it was fine. I danced for a few hours before becoming worn out and sitting down. As I drank some water, I noticed one of the security guards lead a rather drunken girl down some stairs to a private area. It didn't look right to me, so I followed. I had not noticed the private section, a rather dungeon-like area that was built to house the ammunition and gunpowder for the big guns. Thick concrete walls and iron doors. There was another party going on in the chambers below. A security guard at the door at the bottom of the stairs helped get the girl into the room. Preoccupied with guiding the stumbling girl into the room, they hadn't noticed me.

The door opened, and the curtain drew back, revealing a momentary scene of carnage. A man, slouched on a throne on a small stage, a sneer on his face, looked down at some guests and partygoers. Some guests stood in a semicircle, while others, drenched in what looked like blood, found themselves under the guards' control in the center. The curtain fell back, and the door slammed shut. A flash, a glimpse—did I really see this? Was it just a party fantasy, or was it for real? I approached the thick metal door and attempted to open it, only to find it locked from the inside.

A hand gripped my mouth, while an arm encircled me from behind, dragging me to the back of the dimly lit corridor into the dark shadows. The person held me tight and told me to be quiet; he told me I was in danger. My instincts told me to oblige. The door opened again, and the guards came out. One guard went up the stairs while the other stood sentinel anew in front of the door. We both stood there in the shadows, hardly daring to breathe. The noise from the two parties hid our noises, but we had to keep still. The drone from the asynchronous techno beats had a dizzying effect on me. In what seemed like an eternity, the guard returned with another inebriated partygoer, and they all went inside. My attacker released me, grabbed my hand, and dragged me up the stairs. Finally, I could get a good look at who it was. It was my cousin, Vincent.

Vincent is tall and lean, with an almost ethereal presence. He often tousles his dark hair, giving himself a perpetually windswept look. He has piercing blue eyes that seem to see right through people, capturing their essence in his artwork. His attire is eclectic, often comprising bohemian-style clothing that reflects his artistic nature. He hurried me through the dance floor and then out onto the landing jetty.

He said, 'We are taking the boat back to Amsterdam; it is not safe here; they may have seen us.' I followed him to the jetty. The boat was about to leave; it contained some guests already heading back. They looked the worse for partying.

'What the hell is this all about, Vincent?' I demanded, but he just pulled me into the boat. He anxiously glanced at the fort, wondering if someone was following us, and only relaxed when the ferry departed to transport us to Amsterdam.

'To tell you the truth, I don't know. I was at the party, just having a good time like you. I had seen you dance at the party, but I wasn't 100 percent sure it was you. The Treurniet family invited me. But the real reason I came was because I had heard things about the Van Os family. Or at least Fredrick van Os. Something is amiss with that man and his family. They are so wealthy they can get away with anything. They have been able to get away with quite a bit.'

He looked out across the river to Amsterdam and seemed deep in thought. The lights of the city reflected in the choppy waters of the Ij river.

'These people are not the top 1%; they are the top 0.0001%. It's rumored they have more money than Gates, Bezos, or Musk. They keep it hidden; they keep it secret. I'm sure what was going on in that room was not legal, and you don't want to get your reputation mixed up in that. It looked weird when the security guy took that girl down, and when I saw you go after them, I followed. That's all I know; that's all I want to know.'

'Did you see what was going on in the room?' I asked, and he shook his head. 'I don't want to know. Put space between you and them; they are too powerful,' he said. He looked at me earnestly; I knew he really meant it.

We had played together often as children; our parents went on holiday together. We owned a chateau in the south of France. Happy memories. I had not seen Vincent for a while. We sat on the boat at the bow and watched the lights of Amsterdam come closer to us. I snuggled up to him as I was getting a little cold. We sat in silence.

I put my hands over the side and let the cold water of the river Ij flow between my fingers. It was as if I could feel a connection with the sailors on board the ships that used to moor at Pampus. So close to their home and yet so far. I had a vivid vision of a young man in the ship's hold. He is in his hammock, sick and dying. He can almost hear Amsterdam in the distance, but he knows he will never see it or see his family waiting on the quay. Did Hemingway once say that a man dies twice: once on his deathbed and again when the last person he ever knew passes away, leaving him forgotten?

I could just imagine sailors from around the world making this same journey for hundreds of years. I could almost see the forest of ship masts as they jostled to deliver their precious cargo of spices and wares.

At the landing pier by the Amstel Hotel, we went ashore. Vincent hugged me and kissed me on the forehead.

'Stay safe, favorite cousin,' he said, and he was gone.

I am a member of the Korps National Politie, and I am not just going to walk away from a potential crime scene. But what exactly did I see? Could I risk my reputation by drumming up an entire SWAT squad? This time I was not in a tuxedo but in a very nice Audrey Hepburn esque black dress. And then to arrest probably the richest family on the planet based on a hunch? I considered going back on my own and arresting twenty guards and thirty extremely wealthy people. I concluded that this would be against protocol, especially since I was wearing the wrong earrings and shoes. So, I dodged a bullet (maybe literally) and decided to regroup with a better plan.

The next day, I returned to Pampus with the excuse of having lost my keys at the party. The concierge at Pampus was very nice. He informed me the party had cleaned up from the previous night's and left early in the morning. He told me they were very generous and did an amazing job of cleaning up. 'I've never seen the fort so spotless,' he said. 'It was as if they had never been here'. They even took the trash with them. They had their own crew. Very professional, and they said little. He allowed me to explore on my own.

I headed to the party room in the basement and opened the heavy metal door. Inside was pitch dark, so I turned on the lights. Rows of sterile neon lights lit up the grey concrete space. It was completely empty. On one side, there was a stack of chairs. There were no thrones, curtains, or party accessories present. There was a garbage bin in one corner. It was empty; a fresh bag awaited open-mouthed.

What happened to that inebriated girl? Was she okay? Was it all just a game? Or did something happen to her?

'Talk to me, whoever you are.' I whispered, as if the girl's presence was still in the room, 'Tell me your story.' I looked around but could find nothing. In my mind, I attempted to arrange the stage, the throne, and the location of the girl within the semicircle of people.

On the floor, I saw a small red dot. A mere pinprick, hardly noticeable on the cold gray linoleum. I took out a sample kit from my bag, and with a Q-tip, I placed the red dot into a test tube. I sealed the evidence bag.

Back at the office, the report from the coroner had arrived concerning the five mummified victims. In a long, rambling analysis, the coroner concluded DNA samples showed the victims were related and that a rare hereditary condition similar to progeria, also known as Hutchinson-Gilford syndrome or Werner syndrome, likely caused their deaths. Despite having the exact opposite symptoms, the victims had remained remarkably young throughout their long lifetimes. The blood tested negative for toxins. The coroner confirmed natural causes were the official cause of death. On a side note, he added we should all consider ourselves fortunate to have this disease, and he suggested we call it the Dorian Gray Syndrome. Captain Der Burg had left a post-it note on the file. 'Close this up.'

I processed the files, wrote my report, and then archived the evidence. After spending nearly a full day processing the files, I sat back, looked at the cardboard box containing the files, and held a small plastic bag containing a test tube and a Q-tip with a small red dot on it. Should I drop this in the box to be lost forever, or should I do something with it? I held it delicately between my two fingers above the grave-like box. Was it blood? Was it paint? What happened to that inebriated girl?

I stood there, leaning over the box, the plastic evidence bag in between my two fingers. I didn't want to pursue it, run all the tests, and risk the captain's ire. But I hesitated to let go. Was this the only remaining trace of some poor Euro-trash tourist?

I allowed the specimen bag to fall into the box like debris, then sealed it with a lid, much like a coffin. I took it to the archive and signed off on the chain of evidence.

Back at my desk, I looked at the pile of folders. They were prints from digital files sent to me from The New York State Library in Albany. Next to it sat a fat white cat, adorned with Delft Blue drawings and patterns on its body. It surveyed me contemptuously, bored.

This is my imaginary cat. It turns up whenever I'm having one of my "melancholy phases." Winston Churchill called his depression a black dog. I have a white and Delft Blue cat.

When I have a melancholy phase I feel all happiness, pleasure, meaning, and worth just drain out of me. It felt as though the weight of gravity had increased, drawing the lightness of existence from my soul and onto the floor.

I have learned to identify the triggers. I have medications, but I don't always need them.

One episode was when I was with friends at an elegant restaurant in the Hamptons. We were having fun. I saw a very preppy man in his sixties with his trophy wife. They both looked bored with living and irritated with each other. Their clothes were expensive. They sat in front of their haute cuisine food, picking at it as if there was a conundrum about eating delicious food and staying fashionably thin. However, their thinness did not equate to youthfulness, but to gauntness. It felt like to lose weight, they had sacrificed their joy and happiness.

Then the waiter brought a dish to their table. The waiter served a delicate sea bass filet with a dill sauce and two haricot verts. Two. The man looked at it with disgust, made a sarcastic comment, and waved it away. The waiter acknowledged it with a small bow and removed the culinary masterpiece. To be tossed into a garbage pail. The man continued his prosaic conversation with his jaded wife. I interrupted the waiter as he was heading back to the kitchen, insisting that I wanted the sea bass. He said he would have a fresh one prepared for me, but I insisted on having that dish. He shrugged his shoulders and gave it to me. I said aloud how delicious it looked and was exquisitely prepared. I sampled every part of the fish in the most exhibitionist way possible. I made sure that the man knew that I was enjoying his delicious fish dish!

I was proud that someone was appreciating the fish, respecting the chef, and ending with gratitude rather than rejection from a bland man.

I hated the arrogance of the man. Why did they not respect the entire process that had brought him that wonder? Life took billions of years to create this magnificent creature. It required immense courage and risk-taking to seize and introduce this creature to the market. The culinary and cultural history evolved over centuries, shaping the recipe and the chef's skills to prepare and cook this meal. The experience and hospitality of the waiter attended to the man's needs. It was wafted away to be tossed into a garbage pail.

And at that moment I felt the gravity of life getting heavier, joy and the innocence of happiness collapsing like a souffle. That couple's indifference made me angry, and unresolved anger leads to sadness. I got through the evening, but then, disgusted with the lightness of everything and its insignificance,

I went to bed for a week.

Another episode was when I ordered a glass jug online before realizing it would take three weeks to arrive from China. I periodically tracked the package's container on its sea voyage. The Ever Given ship's stranding caused the package to become stuck in the Suez Canal. Finally, it got to Amsterdam, where a careless delivery guy tossed the package onto the marble hall floor, and the delicate glass jug cracked. The fragile glass jug had journeyed thousands of miles, only to succumb to its sloppy, careless destruction. I looked at the broken glass jug. Thin, delicate, and vulnerable. It had made a heroic journey from sand to artisanal glassblower to an epic sea voyage, only to be smashed by laziness and indifference. I went to bed for a week.

The doctors call it cyclothymia, my fat Delft Blue cat.

What triggered the Blue Delft cat's visit this time? Was it the presence of a bloodstain? Was it the insignificance and fate of the intoxicated girl that mattered? The arrogance of the wealthy partygoers? I started feeling the cat's presence on the boat back from Pampus. I looked at the skyline of Amsterdam Central Station, where centuries before, ships' masts were metronomes to the beat of the river. I missed every one of the souls who had lived here. Who were they, and what were their dreams? What did they do, and what happened to them? I thought about the sailors dying alone in a ship's hull from some unknown foreign tropical disease. The butchers, carpenters, and merchants. Rope-makers, sail-makers, cooks, and tailors. Beggars and thieves. From the very beginning of the city's history, many of the first residents were refugees, travelers, or immigrants. What were their stories? Is it fair that those stories are gone forever? So many.

When the global pandemic hit and the tourists stayed away, I would wander the streets of Amsterdam during curfew. Early in the morning, I imagined myself wandering the canals in 1700. My apartment was located in one part of the Herengracht, where the canal walls were undergoing renewal. The scene resembled what it would have looked like two centuries ago, with the removal of trees and the ban on car parking. It was beautiful. And in the early morning mist that enveloped the Noordermarkt, I could see the ghostly shapes of people buying and selling. I imagined, for a second, that I could see the ghosts of Amsterdam's past.

I grabbed a pile of files and went home. With the help of Hiro, some small blue lithium tablets, and the generous indulgence of Dutch labor laws, I spent the next few days in bed. Hiro had hidden the knives, the sleeping pills (which were actually iron supplements and my contraceptive pills; I don't think his Dutch is as good as he thinks it is), and, for some reason, the hair dryer. It was endearing, though. I told him suicide was the last thing I would ever do, and he said that wasn't funny.

But he also lets me get on with it. He brought the occasional light snack, cleaned up, and kept out of my way. I'm fortunate to have him. I had learned that distraction is part of my cognitive-behavioral therapy, so when I had the energy, I started reading the files from Albany.

They were the official records, contracts, sales receipts, and general proclamations of lawyers, politicians, and merchants kept in an archive since the start of that Dutch colony called New Amsterdam in the 1600s. This place, now called Manhattan, helped give the Dutch a foothold in the vast new world. The originals and transcripts, which were laboriously translated from the Dutch that contemporary Dutch can hardly read, were present. I followed the long, elegant bows and curves of the writing with my finger, attempting to sketch the graceful shapes while contemplating the identity of the writer, his aspirations, and his plans.

What was I looking for? I was opportunistic, seeing if there were patterns. I needed to create a family tree of the wealthy families of the Old and New Amsterdam, and hidden in the writing were its origins. Did the seed of all this wealth really start here, and could I follow this path through to today? Could I uncover the true source of power, potential corruption, and the rumors that have surrounded me throughout my life? Where these whispers and gossip we rich children would share with each other about our families while the adults drank martinis or spent weekends away, true?

And then there it was—my first clue. A curly script spelled out the name Van Os. The more I looked, the more I found the name Frederick Van Os. I took notes from the moment his name first appeared until the point at which Frederick Os disappeared. Or a son or daughter took over. Dutch women, whether they were wives or daughters, achieved emancipation years ahead of their global counterparts.

I followed his trail. He bought cotton, tobacco, and spices. As his capital resources grew, I could see his interests move toward insurance and real estate. Van Os was successful. He was also very fortunate. He never insured ships that made safe journeys, always preferring to insure ships that would later shipwreck or, as often occurred, simply disappear.

There was something even more peculiar about the situation. Something was wrong, but I could not put my finger on it. My training as a historian kicked in, and I tried to imagine a day in the life of Van Os in the 1600s. He was in Manhattan, where he purchased various goods, commodities, and spices and then accepted his cargo from a ship named 'The Flute' that was sailing from Amsterdam. A few days later, he was in Amsterdam. He bought some options in insurance on 'The Flute.' He paid a premium price, which was higher than the price he would have paid before the ship left. Why would he do that?

But that was not right. It took a minimum of six weeks for messages to travel across the Atlantic. Often longer. How could he be in Manhattan, accepting goods from The Flute, only to find himself in Amsterdam a few days later? Knowing that The Flute had safely arrived, but weeks before anybody in Amsterdam would know, underwriting the insurance on The Flute was a safe bet. Easy money.

Was there an error in the contracts? Human error easily led to confusion between the Gregorian and Julian calendars. Yet I found more; Van Os was darting back and forth across the Atlantic as if by magic. Maybe it was a different Van Os. He had a relative named Johannes with whom he conducted the business. However, the knowledge they shared was a six-week unfair advantage. It was too striking and occurred too frequently to be a coincidence.

The Delft Blue cat licked its paw, then jumped off the corner of my bed to disappear into thin air. I cracked my laptop, then started making what I love best, a timeline. The distraction helped; I was feeling better.

Back at the office, there was a fresh case waiting for me on my desk. It was about the disappearance of Harry Fenema. Prof. Harry Theodorus Maria Fenema was a specialist in astrophysics, one of the world's most prominent experts on time theory, and the author of a definitive work on music theory. He lived a life as a recluse, so it was unclear when he had exactly "disappeared." His cleaner, who would work once every two weeks, was the one who discovered his disappearance. I grabbed the file and went to his house, a remote farm in Broek in Waterland.

The house was isolated. The roads were lined with willows that had been pollarded (pruned down to stumps—it's a thing here)—stumpy trees with afros acting as windbreaks. The land is flat and green, and the occasional church spire punctures the horizon. An old sail windmill stood to the north, serving as a stark contrast to the ubiquitous modern wind turbines. It was a classic Dutch landscape. I nearly missed the driveway to the house, as it was hidden by trees and had disappeared into the flatness of everything.

The house stood alone in a cow-filled field, akin to an oasis, encircled by trees. A low mist filled the fields and surrounded the house. I had to wait for someone from the local police to arrive with keys so we could break the seals on the locked house. It was remote here. The Vermeer clouds drifted over, teasing with some rays of the sun. Amsterdam was not far away, and yet this seemed so dreary. All you could hear was the wind and the occasional melancholic cow. The house was a single-story building, with rooms built in the attic for sleeping. The style was classic Dutch. Somber, sober, efficient. It was proper, conventional, even pious. The Calvinist Puritan influence. All the houses had the same green shutters, and the windows were painted white with green trim.

The local policeman, a corpulent, no-nonsense man with a large nicotine-stained walrus mustache, arrived and was surprised to find only me. That meant calling the station for some reason before he let me in. Inside was a complete juxtaposition to the outside. Bleak and dreary on the outside, the inside, unlike most somber and dull Dutch farmhouses, was full of cultural and artistic artifacts. Masks from Africa, Indonesian puppets. Japanese musical instruments. A grand piano. The house exuded refinement and eclecticism, not merely a collection of haphazardly placed items, but a coherent whole. I couldn't quite put my finger on it, but then I realized he had subtly matched the colors. There was a flow; it was telling a story. Fennema had style.

We had checked the house but found no evidence of a crime, no struggle, and no blood spilled. I always felt nervous about poking around on someone else's property. What if he just walks in from being away? His laptop was on the dining table, so I put on some gloves and pressed the power button. The system prompted me for a password, so I clicked 'forgot password' and received a prompt to send a text to his mobile for permission. I immediately heard a ping from a mobile phone located somewhere in the house. It seemed to come from upstairs. I located the phone, but I could not unlock it to view the text message. It was strange that he had not taken his phone with him. Nobody does that unless he has more than one phone, but it was next to his bed. It was his main phone.

I opened the cupboard and then let out a scream; there was a desiccated skeleton with a painted face, holding a spear, staring back at me. The walrus-mustache came running up the stairs but then re-holstered his gun. The skeleton was just something from Africa that Fennema was storing in the cupboard.

'I drew my gun; I will have to write a report now,' the mustache said. He was not happy.

I calmed my nerves and apologized. I went back to look at the laptop and tried a few generic passwords. The walrus mustache told me to try the password, "Blackhole." I tried it, and it worked!

How did you know that? I asked. He showed me the post-it note on the table next to the laptop. It said, "password: Blackhole."

'So, you are a detective, huh?' he said. 'How's that working out for you?'

I asked him if he knew Jaap van der Geintje, and he confirmed he did, leaving me feeling a mix of surprise and lack of surprise, which was odd.

I rummaged through Fennema's emails. The last two weeks were unread. He efficiently sorted emails into folders for friends, work, general household, and colleagues. He had set up rules in his email app to sort the emails as they came in. I copied his contact list and calendar and emailed them to myself. I labeled and bagged the laptop as evidence, and then I looked around the house some more, and then I said I was leaving.

'Will you be able to find your way back on your own, Detective?' the walrus mustache asked.

Back at the station, I started crunching the data. I emailed Fennema's friends from my email account, explaining the situation and asking if they had heard from him or had any useful information. I inquired about the last time they had seen or heard from him. All the responses I received essentially followed the same pattern. Fennema was beloved in his fields of work but was a recluse, had few friends, and they were one of the few people he contacted. All 525 of them. The same was true for his 1326 colleagues. Although the public perceived him as a troglodyte, in reality, he was socially active. He was just a private person.

He had left everything in his will to a scientific institute; nobody had taken out any insurance policies on his life. All the emails seemed to be friendly and upbeat. He was not a member of any suicide clubs or kinky websites. His parents were dead, and he had no relatives. He had disappeared into thin air.

He had traveled a lot, but Covid had planted him firmly in his house, something he embraced. He completed work projects and held Zoom meetings with colleagues and friends. His last Zoom meeting was with a professor of physics in Canada. The professor had recorded it, and he sent me a copy. Fennema chatted with the professor about astrophysics in jargon beyond my capacity, but his tone and body language were of a man full of life and happy with his circumstances.

As part of the process, I searched the police database for similar cases and found five. All eminent physicists. They were solitary, possessing minimal familial and social connections. Over the past two years, they had simply vanished from sight. No one took any money. They shared another trait, they had all written articles about the physics of time. I was reminded of Virginia Woolf, who one day went for a walk and was never seen alive again. Eventually, someone found her body. Will my five be found again?

I entered all the data into my database and began searching for any similarities. Eventually, I found a name, Pieter Oetgens, a New York philanthropist, who had contact with them all, usually about funding grants. His name was associated with an American-Dutch cultural society, which included the Os family as one of its primary sponsors. I was not looking for any connection to the Os family, but there it was.

The line of investigation made little sense to the captain, so I split the investigation into two: the Os version and the non-Os version. For the rest of the week, I followed as many leads as I could on the non-Os version. That weekend, I flew to New York to pursue the Van Os version—off the books.

Chapter 3

Hiro flew to New York before me to get my flat ready, which meant stocking the fridge, cleaning up, and taking any clothes I might want to wear. Also, clean up after my sister Thea, with whom I share the flat and who is a mess. Throughout the week, I made significant progress in the Fennema case, which included creating a psychological profile of lifestyles and indication of suicide ideation.

I flew out from Schiphol in the early evening. The plane flew in a beautiful curve, following the horseshoe shape of Amsterdam's canals. I marveled at the way Amsterdam was first built. Because of the city's congestion and health issues, the city council members made the unprecedented decision to expand the city to five times its original size. They built three wide canals in a semicircle around the city's core. They gave the canals dignified names like the Prinsengracht—the Princess Canal, Keizersgracht—the Emperor's Canal, or the poshest, the Herengracht, the Gentleman's Canal, in a stroke of marketing brilliance.

The city council sold the land between the canals to build houses. Nearly three thousand buildings arose quickly, each balanced on top of forty twenty-meter-long wood poles. This was necessary to access the solid clay beneath the mud on which Amsterdam rested. If you could lift Amsterdam up and flip it, it would look like a forest of Scandinavian pine trees.

Envision this: a king lays claim to the land where you reside and labor. Your identity and survival are inextricably linked to this land. The king believes God ordained his ownership, thus justifying it. The land belongs to the king, since, in his view, God created it. He had a divine right.

However, what if you and your people were the ones who created the land? Through your hard work, you built dikes and drained the marshes, creating an entirely new piece of land where none existed before. How could any king ownership over this land when it was your tribe's labor that transformed it into what it is today? You would believe this land belongs to you.

This once uninhabitable marshland became a independent space where freedom of thought and expression flourished. People from various backgrounds, such as philosophers, entrepreneurs, refugees, and adventurers, flocked to this unique place. It became a sanctuary and a platform for spreading new ideas. Establishing freedom in this way makes it irrevocable. People came from all over to seek sanctuary and share their beliefs, ultimately leaving a lasting impact on the development of our modern world.

On any day, if you listen carefully, you can still hear Amsterdam has a heartbeat. Pile drivers thump, thump, thump as they push piles through the mud to the solid ground, building yet another structure. This rhythm has continued unabated since the construction of the first permanent houses in Amsterdam.

Amsterdam also has a fragrance, a signature perfume. The city of Amsterdam boasts the largest cocoa port in Europe, home to the Heineken brewery that brews hops into beer. As a child, I recall that this cities' scent would shift between chocolate and hops, depending on the direction of the wind and her mood.

Casparus van Houten, a Dutchman, invented chocolate from the cocoa beans. As we flew over the Amsterdam harbor, filled with ships loaded with cacao beans, I found a small chocolate square in my complimentary business class gift bag and nibbled on it.

I'm surprised by the ease with which I can sleep in the business class. I don't understand why people opt for coach travel.

At JFK, I treated myself to a helicopter to the helipad on 30th Street and got to my flat in the meatpacking district in time for a quick shower, and then I hustled my way into a dinner party at the American-Dutch Mutual Exchange Society. It was a haunt of Pieter Oetgens, and I had vaguely heard of it. However, the Dol family is well-known in Amsterdam and New York, so we often received invitations to join and attend events. The society secretary welcomed me, and I signed up for an annual subscription and their newsletter.

I had a reputation in this very rarefied world as being an academic. Some people may even know I provided consultancy services to the authorities. I had, however, kept it a secret that I was a full-blown detective. This was to my advantage on many levels, especially with my work investigating the layers of the rich Amsterdam families. It was an effortless secret to keep; rich people are self-absorbed by nature. In America, I held no authority whatsoever.

When building the first houses in Amsterdam, they adhered to the French tradition of making the fronts and facades removable. This meant that, much like a new trend, you could change your appearance every season to keep up with the latest fashion. This resulted in the fronts of many houses in Amsterdam today being more modern than their backs. However, this quickly grew tiresome, leading to the cessation of the trend. Despite appearing plain and unadorned on the outside, these eclectic facades often concealed enormous wealth within. In times of European wars and revolutions, it was smart not to advertise your wealth. And this is a core tenet of Dutch society. Never show off your wealth; never be ostentatious.

This was not the case in New York. The American-Dutch Society was housed in an elegant townhouse on the Upper East Side, near the Metropolitan Museum of Art. This beautiful New York townhouse had an imposing stone front with a large lobby. A string quartet played polite chamber music as the crowd gathered to sip Champagne and discuss business. Nearly everyone at the event was tall. I introduced myself, pretended to sip the champagne, and then secretly explored the building. The lower floor rooms served as gallery spaces. There were a few portraits of famous Dutch admirals—a sketch of Peter Stuyvesant and a piece of wood that was rumored to be his peg leg. One wall held examples of stocks and shares, issued in Amsterdam, for trade with New Amsterdam through the VOC—the Dutch East India Company.

It was a loud and chaotic party; Dutch isn't ideal for quiet chat, and everyone seemed to be yelling. There was a staircase leading upstairs. I pretended to look for the bathroom. There was a small office, the door almost hidden in the oak paneling of the hallway. It was beautiful, with a window looking out onto the cross street. There were portraits through the ages of famous Dutch traders. There was one that caught my eye. I am not a connoisseur of art, but this looked like a Rembrandt. It had that brushstroke—rough colors, confidence, and audacity. This was a portrait of a man who was not trying to be something else; this was a man who was proud of who he was. He reminded me of someone, but I could not place it.

There was something else. There was a very faint smell of oil paint. That characteristic smell of linseed oil. Despite the man in the portrait donning a 17th-century tradesman's costume, the painting appeared to be contemporary. From my bag, I took out a sample kit—something a girl detective always keeps in her Hermes Birkin handbag—and, using a Q-tip from a test tube, lightly dabbed a small blue patch on the painting. There was a small blue dot on the Q-tip; it was still wet. I was getting quite the small, colorful dot collection. I bagged the specimen and looked at the painting some more. Then I noticed a note next to the painting. It described the place and profession of the portrayed man. New Amsterdam, Merchant. The date—1698—and his name. Frederik Van Os.

Someone placed their hand on my shoulder, and I let out a scream. I scream a lot. I let out a whooping noise, perform a panic dance in one spot, and display jazz hands. It's annoying and embarrassing and appears as immature. I'm trying not to do it, but it's instinctive.

'Oh, I'm sorry,' said the man. 'I didn't mean to startle you.'

I quickly replied, 'I was just looking for the washroom,' realizing immediately that he was not questioning my reason for being in the room. That came across as questionable right away.

'It's a beautiful picture, isn't it?' he said. 'It's on loan from the owners, the family of Frederik Van Os.'

He was a man in his sixties; he looked like a fellow academic, with bifocals and a cultured look to him. I calmed down. 'Yes, it's nice; you have many pictures here,' I replied. 'I love Art.' I said lamely. He smiled and offered his hand. 'My name is Pieter Oetgens,' he said. 'Boudewijna Dol' I said. 'Of the Dol family? he asked. I nodded. He seemed nice, and I felt the urge to ask him if he knew where Fennema was.

He said, seemingly able to read my thoughts, 'Down the hall to the left,' then smiled and left. I wondered what he meant by that until I realized he meant the washroom. I felt a little off-track and jet-lagged. I didn't want to look for confirmation of any bias (and what was that bias anyway?), so I mingled for a while.

I found myself in a small group of Dutch-Americans practicing our Dutch language skills when Oetgens joined us. We chat, and I mentioned that we might have a friend in common, Harry Fennema. Oetgens looked a little puzzled, and when I prompted him on who Fennema was, he said he remembered, but it seemed more like he was being polite. He stated he contacts many individuals daily regarding grants and sponsorships. He asked how Harry was. Oetgens didn't seem to know that Fennema was missing. This seemed like a dead end.

I was about to leave when a very elegant lady in a black dress came over and asked if she could talk to me for a few moments. She looked in her forties and was obviously very wealthy, considering the tasteful pearls and jewelry that she wore. She looked familiar, like Cruella de Vil. We went out to a terrace. I apologized for my fatigue, explaining that I had just arrived from a flight from Europe. She reassured me it would not take long, and her driver would take me home.

'It has been a while since we have met, Boudewijna,' she said. 'I am a friend of the family. Your father and mother used to visit us in the Hamptons. You might not remember me, as you were just a girl, and, in our circles, we meet so many people. We are a large village, really. In reality, we are a small town, but we are wealthy enough to breed like rabbits.

I smiled, but was not sure where she was going with this. She said, 'I saw you at the wedding in Amsterdam and at the party afterward,' as if she'd caught me in the act. I realized then that she was indeed a Van Os.

'I see you were talking to Oetgens. He is an amiable man, but he can be a bit, how should I say, scatty. Let's avoid creating another scandal within the Dol family, similar to the previous one.' She smiled and put her hand on my cheek. She said, 'I'm glad to see you have joined our wonderful Dutch society.' I hope to see more of you. My driver awaits, she said. Then she left. I had been lectured to and then dismissed. Before I knew it, the driver had parked outside and returned me to my flat.

I looked out at the New York skyline. It never ceased to amaze me—the tall buildings and the endlessness of it all. New York was the world's center, like Amsterdam centuries earlier.

I was tired, jet-lagged, and ready to sleep. However, my fatigue did not prevent me from realizing that the elegant lady had threatened and dismissed me. I jotted down a note to follow up on that thought, then collapsed onto the bed. The sounds of the cars and the sirens made the soundtrack to my sleep.

The next day, I went to Chelsea Market to get my essential coffee and croissant. It's my go-to; it grounds me in my New Amsterdam. Fun fact: my flat is on 10th Avenue, which transitions into Amsterdam Avenue around 60th Street. The Dutch influence is obvious throughout this area.

You're curious about the scandal that rocked the Dol family. The first scandal involved Cousin Ferdinand. He was the son of my father's brother. Ferdinand was eccentric. He opted to go into the family business but was unsuccessful at anything; in fact, he was rather a burden.

Like most Dol men, he married a trophy wife, a Russian. His promotion to manager of the Dol Whisky Company distillery on a remote Scottish island did not amuse his socialite wife. Pretty quickly, she would go to London or Paris for a weekend to get her highlights done by 'George' or shop in New York because she had absolutely nothing to wear. Those weekends were often longer than actual weeks and more frequent than Ferdinand could tolerate.

Soon his wife departed, never returned, and vanished from everyone's sight. Ferdinand said she had taken a sum of money with her, as well as some jewelry and other valuables. We whispered our concerns, expressed our sympathy to Ferdinand, and agreed that he would be better off without her before we all moved on. A few years later, Ferdinand introduced a new pet whisky called Galla fèin-fhìn, which he wanted to age for ten years. It was a side project, and he seemed to have settled into his role at the distillery.

After a few years, one employee tasted the progress of this new elixir and tap off a small dram. It was sour and had a musty taste. When he opened the lid, he discovered Ferdinand's wife, replete with a mink coat and diamonds and pearls. Galla fèin-fhìn means selfish bitch in Scottish Gaelic.

With the help of our expensive and skilled lawyers, Ferdinand successfully refuted the accusations by denying any wrongdoing and claiming his wife was connected to the Russian mob.

Another scandal occurred while I was away at college. One son of the elite families date-raped Thea while she was attending a party in the Hamptons. My father kept it a secret from me to avoid causing publicity for the family, but his fury was palpable. He resolved to hold the responsible individual accountable and threatened the family with dire consequences. A moderator was present, and they held secret meetings. From what Thea told me, at one meeting, something happened, and my father suddenly became silent and timid. He implored Thea to forget about it and to move on. This was not typical of my father, and the incident negatively impacted his relationship with both my mother and Thea. Thea accepted some compensation and apologies, but from my perspective, she seemed to go from that innocent, joyful child in a secret garden to an introverted and insecure person. Rumors circulated afterward, accusing Thea of being at fault and leading the boy astray. She was troublesome, a harlot to steer clear of. This infuriated me, and although I knew I had to let it rest, I vowed that if the opportunity arose, I would do something about it. I searched for a method of revenge. Insider trading provided my entry point.

Growing up, I had a healthy distrust of the rich families we associated with. They seemed nice on the surface, but even a child could see the Byzantine codes of conduct and hear the Machiavellian gossip. I thought it was the inevitable toxic result of entitlement and privilege.

My sister endured trauma, and my family faced threats. She was a mere inconvenience to some rich family; my father was someone who needed to be dealt with and managed. A nuisance.

But my sister is a wonderful, sweet, and generous human being, and my father is a hard-working, highly ethical, and responsible man.

In my world, they were not to be marginalized for someone else's self-importance.

My mother instilled in me the trait of waiting, planning, and always seeking revenge. In our family, we refer to this as Pascal's Vendetta. Years may pass, but the outcome is inevitable; there is a debt to settle. My father and sister refrained from disclosing specifics, and I preferred not to reopen old wounds. My mother understood, and she helped me where she could. She knew how to play the long game. She also desired retribution, and I agreed to act as her proxy.

I am a fan of the Art of War, and according to Sun Tzu, to wage war, you first need to understand your opponent. But my enemy was obscure. I knew that I would have to build a road map of the power that these families have. However, digging around in elitists' secrets is something you need to do carefully. My tactic was to feign interest in other things and glean information peripherally.

I emailed Pieter Oetgens; he seemed to be an innocuous member of the elitist club and maybe an easy backdoor into their world. I asked him if I could talk about Harry Fenema, as we were concerned about his whereabouts. He responded quickly, and he invited me to his penthouse on 5th Avenue. I discovered through some Googling that he was a wealthy man who dedicated his retirement to philanthropy. He mostly engaged in scientific pursuits, exhibiting an eclectic set of interests.

The lobby of the apartment block was, of course, luxurious. The doorman buzzed me up, and I went to the 16th floor in the private elevator of the penthouse suite. All the residential buildings on 5th Avenue are the same height, the maximum length of a fire engine ladder. Oetgens met me at the lift door, which opened directly into his apartment. He was scatterbrained and had difficulty keeping to the subject, but I let him ramble. His maid made tea, and he practiced his stumbling Dutch on me. I complimented him. He promised to forward some emails he had from Fenema, and I padded my backstory as a concerned friend of Fenema, hoping that any clues would be at least comforting, if not helpful.

I admired his apartment, and he informed me he owned the only vineyard in Manhattan. He then led me to his roof patio, a glass atrium filled with stubby vines bearing grapes. It had beautiful vistas of Central Park, but Oetgens potted between his plants, pruning the leaves, jaded to the view. He lectured on grape types and seasonality. The vines had been there for a while, and the entire atrium was climate-controlled. He told me he was doing science experiments with different soil—terroir—seeing how it affected the taste. He said that from a commercial point of view, each bottle of wine he made would cost tens of thousands of dollars. But he was an experimenter, not a wine merchant.

It seemed precious to me, so I let him babble on about it. I noticed five FedEx boxes near the door, which were opened and still contained a substance similar to soil. Oetgens had received them from Amsterdam. While Oetgens was busy pruning, I secretively pulled out another sample kit and took a sample of dirt with a Q-tip from the bag. I quickly took a photograph with my phone of the label, hoping to get a tracking number or the address of the sender. Why was dirt being sent to him from the Netherlands?

'What are you doing?' he asked. I don't think he had seen me taking a sample or photo, but he saw I was near the bags. 'I was just looking at this terroir,' I said, 'and of course this beautiful atrium is so special.' He smiled briefly, politely, but his demeanor had changed. He simply glanced at me before suggesting that it might be time for me to depart, as he had other obligations to fulfill. His manner was no longer friendly, but businesslike. His mood had changed. I had done something wrong; the bags meant something to him other than dirt, and he was not sure if he had been careless or if he was being played. I acted charming and played up the ditzy girl routine about going shopping and looking forward to going to the Hamptons.

He walked me to the elevator, and we said our goodbyes. Whatever had happened, he was suspicious, but why?

I now had three Q-Tip samples: red, blue, and black. I was collecting quite the rainbow of mistrust.

Back at my apartment, Hiro had cleaned and packed my bag for my flight back to Amsterdam. I assumed he had already left to get the Amsterdam apartment ready. I called some friends, and we went out for a meal in the West Village. After an exciting week that was catching up with me, I excused myself and left for an early night. Shortly after I got to my apartment, two rather bulky bodyguards were at my door. They were of the type I had seen at the wedding in Amsterdam.

'How did you get past the doorman?' I asked. They said that someone wanted to see me, and I would come with them. I responded I would prefer not to accompany them unless they could identify the person. One guard said he was Santa Claus, then they each grabbed me under my arm, lifted me up, frog marched me out of the building, and threw me into the back of a big black Lincoln Navigator, license number HFV-9 something-something.

I know my cars. When I was 12, I had this fear that a car would run me over and not know what type of car it was or the number plate, so I memorized all the different types and practiced remembering number plates. I was a strange child.

As the car sped up northward along the Henry Hudson Parkway, I found myself seated between these two silverback gorillas. They were wearing the same black suits and sunglasses (at eleven o'clock at night). They were wearing the same earpieces that the secret service used for communication. There was a slight smell of sulfur in the car.

'Did you just fart?' I asked the gorillas, but they just ignored me.

'Gross,' I scolded them.

I knew that the Henry Hudson Parkway went over the East River on the Henry Hudson Bridge, where it empties into the Hudson River. The Bronx receives the traffic from the bridge at a location known as Spuyten Duyvil. So Spuyten Duivel means 'to spite the devil' in old Dutch. The term originated when Peter Stuyvesant, the Dutch Governor of Manhattan, dispatched Anthony Van Corlaer, one of his trumpeters, to alert the Dutch in the Bronx about the British invasion. As no ferryman was available, he crossed the East River by swimming—to spite the devil—and drowned.

The Henry Hudson Bridge has two layers; the top deck empties into the Bronx, and the bottom layer feeds Manhattan. Slowing and stopping at the bridge's apex, the Lincoln came to a halt. The gorillas exited the vehicle, dragging me along with them. They just stood there; one of them talked into their earpiece. We waited for several minutes, during which the gorillas ignored my inquiries. Then a police car stopped the traffic, and two cops got out. As they approached the Lincoln, the gorillas abruptly dropped me, got back in the car, and drove off.

'Thank you, officers,' I said when they got to me. 'The license plate number is HFV-9098, and it's a black Lincoln Navigator.' The police officers smiled, grabbed me under the arms, and threw me over the side of the bridge into the river. And that's where my story started.

So there I was, hurtling downward toward the East River. I will freeze-frame this plummet halfway to discuss some important details. The Henry Hudson Bridge is 143 ft above the river. The average body falls at a rate of 32 feet per second, with the rate increasing by 32 feet every second. It would take me about 2.5 seconds to reach the bottom. So I would be traveling at about 68 mph when I hit the water. If I were to collide with solid ground, the story would end abruptly here. But water is different. A jump from the Golden Gate Bridge, 220 feet above the water, usually means death. The George Washington Bridge, standing at 212 feet, also poses a significant risk. However, a trained diver could finagle this fall from the Hudson Bridge and survive. The trick is to land feet first and at a slight angle. However, as I fall, I am making a whooping sound, performing a panic dance, and using jazz hands.

Anyway, this seems like a perfect time to recap what I have learned so far. First, we had the five mummifications. The Amsterdam wedding tied them to one of the tribe's richest families, which was strange but interesting.

Then there was the inebriated girl and that bizarre scene I witnessed on Pampers Island. Was that red dot just some paint or was it blood? Was there a story behind that?

Was the strange activity in the historical documents, where Van Os seemed to traverse the Atlantic as if he lived in modern times connected? Then, there was a portrait of Van Os from the sixteenth century, in which the oil paint was still wet.

Then the disappearance of the five leading scientists and artists. Again, while only superficially linked to the elitists, small connections still trace back to the Van Os family, a prominent faction within the elite tribe. And the strange Oetgens and the bags of dirt at his winery. What was that all about?

That's besides the fact that someone threw me off a bridge.

My excessive focus on finding evidence to support my bias also worried me. As a detective, my training instructs me to seek the truth, not to harbor prejudice. Was I simply being paranoid just because someone had thrown me off a bridge? Was I overreacting? Well, there is only one way to find out; I will unfreeze myself and continue my investigation. Wish me luck.

Splash!

Chapter 4

Everything went dark, and cold and wet. I became disorientated. I felt drowsy, felt a heavyweight on top of me. There was noise, like water splashing and someone shouting. I needed to sleep. Just let me sleep for a few minutes. Then there was silence and warmth. I just lay there. Had I passed out? It was dark and quiet, and I felt strangely content. I was no longer wet and cold but resting on a bed that was dry and warm. I felt a peace and tranquility wash over me, like acceptance.

I lay there calmly. I ran my fingers over the sides of the bed. A wooden wall enclosed the bed on three sides, like a coffin, but I felt I could sit up with no problem. Was I in a hospital? I felt no injuries, no trauma. The wood felt unfinished, unpainted, roughly cut by hand, and un-sanded. A splinter got stuck in my finger. I heard noises outside, like children chattering. I scraped at the wood with a fingernail. There was a smell of nutmeg, and my finger had nutmeg powder on it. A chicken clucked outside. I tried pushing the walls, then realized that one side was a curtain, so I pushed a little, and light streamed in through the cracks. I pulled the curtains carefully apart.

I was in a bedstee, an old-fashioned bed that was more like a wardrobe that contained a bed. The room was old and in the style of a sixteenth-century Dutch house, as depicted in a Vermeer painting. The furniture, of varying sizes, was handmade, and someone had pinned the upholstery on with large tacks. Crude plaster covered the walls, and uneven Delft blue tiles lined the bottom of the walls. There was a thick rug on a table with a pewter jug and bowl. The windows had what seemed like cheaply made glass, with impurities and uneven thickness that blurred the view outside. The floor was rough cut wooden planks with a simple rug.

Besides that, there was little in the room, besides a chicken, which pecked optimistically at the wooden floor. It was not full of modern attributes like devices and posters and lamps. There was a cross on the wall. The room looked newly built using old techniques and common basic materials. Part of the plaster from the wall had already peeled off and I could see the use of grass reed underneath as a frame.

Some children ran into the room. They were wearing traditional Dutch clothes, petticoats, and clogs. They ignored me and ran about, a small dog barking at their heels. I climbed out of the bedstee. The children just ran around a small table in the middle of the room and then ran out of the room again and down some stairs.

There was a smell. It was a mix of smoke and cooking, and what seemed to me the street smells from my travels in India and farmland. There were noises from the street that were odd. Not that of cars and traffic, but of people shouting, the sound of animals. Horses, chickens, goats. I looked out of the window. Outside was a canal. There were barges carrying large flaxen bags. A man rolled a barrel down the canal side. Everyone wore 17th-century costumes. A boy pee'd into the canal from a bridge.

There were street sellers with apples and onions, fish, and meats. Horses pulled barges and carriages with people. I recognized the canal. It was the Leidsegracht in Amsterdam. But it looked different, newer. There were no trees or cars parked along the canal sides. Some houses were still in construction.

The children ran back into the room. One child brushed against me without stopping. He didn't even seem to notice me. I followed them downstairs. There were more people in the rooms downstairs. There were maids cleaning. An old man sat reading some papers in the corner, smoking a clay pipe. A woman, doing some needlepoint, stood up and came over to me.

'Hello. Who are you?' she said. 'Can I help you?'. Her Dutch had a strange accent, as if from Belgium or some eastern province. I didn't know what to say. The man with the pipe came over to me. He seemed a little confused. 'My name is Boudewijna Dol,' I said.

'*Ach ja,*' said the man, collecting himself. '*Sy is Hendricks' dochter. Sy quam gisteravond laat aen. Vergeeft my, lieve, ick vergat u te seggen, dat ick haer hier ghenoodicht heb om te verblijven. Sy is van Londen herwaerts ghecomen. Ick heb Hendrick belooft wel op haer te passen. Hoe was uw vaert over het Kanael, mijn lieve? Ick hope dat het u niet te seer vermoeiende was.*'

'This is Hendricks' daughter. She arrived late last night. I'm sorry dear, I forgot to tell you, I invited her to stay here. She is visiting from London. I promised Hendrick I would take care of her. How was your sail across the Channel, my dear? I hope not too exhausting?'

He had the same accent. Some words seemed more like an affect. It was not modern Dutch.

I couldn't answer because I was totally confused. I decided to go with the flow and just smiled.

The language they spoke was old Dutch. I easily understood it, though they occasionally used French or Latin words, and the grammar sounded convoluted and forced to me. But I could follow the context. I faked my Dutch with English words to show I was from somewhere else. In Amsterdam, everybody was from somewhere else.

'Ah, Hendricks' daughter!' said the woman. 'How is Hendrick and the Family? We have not seen them for a year! You must be hungry. Let us prepare some food for you! My, you have grown. Is your husband accompanying you?' said the woman. 'I'm afraid the plague took Boudewijna's husband, Theo,' said the man. I feigned sadness. One thing was for sure, this man was covering for me, and hiding something from his wife.

'Trouble yourself, not with food, wife', he said. 'I am taking Boudewijna to meet some business partners of her husband to conclude some transactions. And I'm afraid we must make haste. There will be sustenance there. Wife, since you're a similar size, lend Boudewijna a dress and some underskirts; the port held up her luggage.

The wife obediently obeyed and brought me something to change into. I could feel the patriarchal social dynamic, his command, and her immediate obedience. I changed clothes quickly. The cloth was a little rough and itchy to my skin, and it was heavy, but I felt I needed to be more inconspicuous. My clothes were too modern for this Christian society, whatever this was. The clogs were hard to my spoilt soft feet, but the long dress covered my sneakers, so I kept them on. I left my undershirt and underwear on, to protect my skin from the itchy fabric.

After I had finished dressing, the man called to me. 'Come, my dear, let's walk together and I will make the introductions.' He grabbed my arm and hastened me out of the house into the street, leaving his confused but obedient wife behind. The street overwhelmed me. I had thought, until now, that this was an elaborate joke (and my rich tribe is known for them), but the street was real. The smell from the canal, the people, the smoke. The street was unpaved. There were no 'Amsterdammers', the ubiquitous traffic bollards. There were no lanterns, and almost unbelievably, there were no bicycles.

Whoever had done this paid attention to detail. But why?

'Walk with me', he said. 'My wife knows nothing of you visitants from afar. My name is Kees Van Haverman. I know you are not from this place. These visits happen in our family and for the masters of which we are servants. You are a stranger to these areas. I have seen some visitants from where you come from. You do look familiar to me in some way. Have we met before? Have you been here, have I taken care of you?'

I told him this was my first visit and left it at that. He knew I was not from London. I explained my surprise at being there, saying that someone had pushed me from a bridge, and then suddenly I was here. He thought it was very unusual. He did not seem to grasp that I was from the future, just from somewhere different and exotic. I kept it that way.

He was a kind, old man. Long white beard and mustache stained with tobacco. Unfortunately, like everyone else around me, he had personal hygiene issues and was rather ripe, but that was part of this era I now was in. It calmed me down to think I was with someone who was sympathetic to what was happening, although he had no answers about how it happened, or how I could get back. It also helped me he was family, even though technically I had not yet been born.

The bustling street was a tapestry of life, how I had imagined the Dutch Golden Age. Narrow cobblestone streets, flanked by tall, gabled houses of brick and wood. Many of the houses have large windows adorned with leaded glass and ornate shutters, showcasing the wealth of the merchants who live there.

The canals, lined with wooden posts and small moored boats, are alive with activity. Merchants unload barrels of goods—spices, textiles, and exotic items from the Dutch East Indies—while boatmen call out to one another in a cacophony of Dutch, mixed with other languages like Portuguese and French, reflecting Amsterdam's cosmopolitan character.

Shops open onto the streets, their wares displayed on tables or hanging from awnings. Bakers sell fresh loaves of rye bread, while cheese monger's offer wheels of creamy Edam and Gouda. Fishmongers display herring and eels, their pungent aroma blending with the salty sea air. A vendor wheels a cart of tulip bulbs, a left-over from the recent frenzy of Tulip Mania.

People crowd the street: men in broad-brimmed hats and knee-length breeches, women in modest dresses with aprons and lace collars, and children darting between them, playing games or carrying errands. Farmers and artisans mingle with sailors and traders, their conversations animated as they haggle over prices or share news from distant lands. Life in this era was a street life. People worked and lived locally; there were few offices or factories.

Artisans and craftsmen work in open-door workshops, the rhythmic sound of hammering and sawing blending with the chatter of the crowd. A barber-surgeon's shop displays a sign depicting razors and bandages. An old woman, her head wrapped in a large bandage, was pushed into the shop. She screamed and struggled, fearful of what pain her cure was going to entail.

Above the noise, the bells of the Westerkerk ring out, marking the hour and adding a layer of structure to the otherwise chaotic scene. The air is thick with the smell of tar from shipbuilding yards, mingled with the earthy scents of horses and the occasional whiff of fresh-brewed beer from a nearby tavern.

This Amsterdam street, both orderly and chaotic, brims with energy, a microcosm of a city at the height of its power and prosperity.

He took me to a cafe and we ate some bread and cheese and drank some wine. Something I noticed was that people talked more. The cafe had no music blaring from speakers. Nobody was looking down at a smartphone. People sat around tables and had conversations. There was no bar, just some girls who peddled between the customers and the kitchen, and who collected the money upfront. One girl sent a beggar away who came inside. A richly dressed merchant from Africa sat in the corner and held court.

The bread and cheese were delicious. Cheese was creamy and fresh, and the bread's crust tasted of honey and was crisp and flakey. The bread crumb was soft and flavorful, with olives and rosemary. Wine smelt vinegary for my taste, as I don't drink, but they served me a hot hop ale that was a more light soup that had no alcohol in it. The old man recommended that I don't drink the water. It was not as pure as where I came from; he cautioned me. "Some visitants had become very sick", he informed me. The cafe served a fish pie that had apples baked in it. They served raw onions as a side dish.

I can assure you I was in a daze, totally confused. I felt frightened, a stranger in a strange place. Would those around think me a witch and burn me? An imposter, a spy? First, someone threw me from a bridge, then I awoke in Amsterdam on what the old man had told me was 1664.

His eldest brother, Hans van Haverman, was in Norway, buying wood for sawmills for timber-hungry Europe. Quality ships' masts, he told me.

Johannes told me he had visitors before, but never someone who had arrived accidentally. His master, Van Os, was usually the person who the visitors wanted to talk to. It was always business. They stayed a day or two, never longer, and then simply disappeared again. He said they were mostly from New Amsterdam. I asked if he knew the Van Os family well, and he said yes, they did business with them. They were the richest family he knew and rather manipulating. He worked with other businesses. The Van Os family was too intense and demanding for his taste. He did well working with them, but their capricious behavior often was not worth it.

There was maybe a connection between the records I had found in Albany of Van Os doing business simultaneously in Amsterdam and New Amsterdam. This seemed to be the answer to that puzzle. But it was an answer that created a legion of new questions and puzzles.

After my meal, I felt calmer. I am a historian; it is my core business. It has been my passion since I was a child. I think playing hide and seek in all those fabulous stately homes. I have spent years trying to create an image of what life would be like hundreds of years ago. Specifically studying Amsterdam and the growth of economic liberalism. Then suddenly, here I was, it was all around me. The Golden Age. I began to feel more confident that they would not drag me out into the streets and burn me at the stake. Looking around me, I could see enough crazy people who would make a better target than me. Amsterdam was indeed a melting pot for Europe. A bastion, a safe harbor for diversity. I could see the poverty as well. Beggars and thieves. Shady characters, waiting for an opportunity. Fascination slowly replaced my fear.

I asked if we could go for a walk. I wanted to see more, and Kees agreed. We walked along the canals. It was fascinating to see life in Amsterdam pass me by. No cars, few trees. Everybody seemed to live out in the street, like it was the King's birthday, but this was just any ordinary day. There was a man burning rubbish; a woman urinated in an alley. Further, a man sold apples from a streetcar that he pushed, along with nuts and bottles of gin. A religious parade passed by. I could fill reams of paper with historical notes, but this is not the moment.

Along the edges of the canals, markets thrived. Street vendors sold fresh fish, bread, fruits, and vegetables, while other stalls displayed textiles, pottery, and goods imported from far-flung corners of the globe. The smell of herring, a staple of the Dutch diet, mingled with the aroma of spices. We walked the Prinsengracht and then through the Reguliersgracht to the Herengracht. My apartment was there, and the sandstone façade was there, but new with no marks of pollution. Most of the buildings had changed. It was the same place, but 400 years earlier. Everything changes, nothing stays the same.

The eighty years' war with Spain was over, the Netherlands finally had independence. Soon Johannes said he was tired; his gout was playing up. He had poor health; he said. I felt sorry for him, knowing that modern medicine could quickly remedy his health problems. But could I do anything about that? Had the previous visitors told Boudewijn Dol anything about the future? Soon the Netherlands would face the disaster of a long war with France. It would put an end to the Golden Years. Could I warn Johannes about that? Would that distort history?

We agreed to meet back at his house, and he left me to wander through this wonderful museum exhibit called Amsterdam all on my own. I feared being alone, but I had to figure out what was happening to me. I walked to the Dam and was surprised to see that construction on the Dam Palace, or city hall as it then was, was still underway. There was a crowd standing around what seemed like a pole or some sort of scaffolding. There was a wharf with ships bringing fish, and the weighing house, long demolished in my time, where goods were weighed and taxed. The commerce at the Dam contributed to Amsterdam's wealth as a major trade hub during the Dutch Golden Age. The Bijenkorf and the Kraznapolsky were gone, or to be correct, not yet there. So strange, such iconic buildings for me. Where the Amsterdam stock Exchange is, was the Beurs van Hendrick de Keyser, the original, and world's first, stock exchange. Everything was the same, and yet different.

The Dam was a large, solid structure bridging the Amstel River. By this time, it was not just a functional dam but also a marketplace and gathering spot. The dam regulated the river's water flow, enabling ships to navigate a system of sluices and contributing to the city's thriving trade. Merchant ships filled the nearby Damrak, an inlet of the Amstel River, loading and unloading goods from the far reaches of the world, including spices, textiles, and luxury items. Amsterdam's port was among the busiest in Europe.

The area around the dam had transformed into Dam Square, a busy public square that played host to merchants, citizens, and travelers from around the world. Merchants filled the square with market stalls, goods, and livestock. It was a lively, commercial space where locals and visitors alike conducted business. Local peddlers saw me, and assuming I had money, tried to sell me something. Fruit, strange vegetables, cloth. Where I would be usually see tourists taking selfies, people were working hard trying to make a living. Trying to survive. I guess tourism is a thing of the future.

Some street kids tried to hustle me for money, but I quickly brushed them off and walked further down the Damstraat. I then realized I was walking towards the house of Rembrandt. Could he be there? Could I see him at work?

I stood outside Rembrandt's house, hesitating, but then finally decided and plucked up the courage. I knocked on the door and a young girl answered. 'Is master Rembrandt van Rijn at home?' I asked. She looked a little sheepish and then left, saying nothing, leaving the door a little open. I assumed she had gone to check, so I waited. A few minutes later, she came back and asked in a monotone voice, 'For what is the purpose of this visit? Are you collecting money? If so, Master van Rijn is not at home'

'I am Boudewijna Dol, of the Dol family. Dol Cookies? My father is a wealthy merchant in London. I am interested in commissioning a portrait.' The girl left and then a minute later, the door was thrown open and there was an exuberant Rembrandt with his arms in the air.

'Welcome! My apologies for my maid. Rembrandt van Rijn is my name. How charming to meet you!'

He had a round, full face, and a rugged, weathered appearance. His eyes seemed to convey a mix of curiosity, wisdom, and melancholy. A puggy rounded nose and full lips and thick, curly hair, but worn somewhat long and unruly, that was dark brownish but was already greying. He sported a small goatee and was stout, if not somewhat portly.

I grew up meeting a lot of celebrities, and even though I can get as star-struck as anyone else, I am also desensitized to the glamor and have met plenty of people who are famous and are crushingly boring in real life. But to meet someone famous who is long dead, now real and animated and alive, is a whole new experience. I could ask him a thousand questions about which paintings he really painted, and what were his thoughts, his process. I could ask him about the people he painted, what did they tell him, and what secrets could he reveal?

He gave me a tour of his studio. He was curious about my accent, which I attributed to living abroad with my parents. His studio was full of unfinished paintings, with a painting he was working on an easel next to a window facing north. A cloth was draped over it. The perfect painter's light, the northern lights. Eclectic pieces filled the studio. A water painting from Japan, miniatures from India, a drum, flags, stuffed animals, a suit of armor, a pike. The studio smelt heavily of linseed oil, and a boy was in a room grinding pigments into the oil with a large glass Muller. Some apprentices worked on side details in his paintings, or on works of their own.

We discussed the details of the portrait which would be of my 'father'. How much would it cost? As my father would only visit Amsterdam at certain intervals, how long would it take? He proposed he would write a letter to my father with the details. I felt he was uncomfortable doing business with a woman. I agreed to the letter and said I would return the next day to pick it up. Trying to act as subservient as possible, I asked politely if I could see what he was working on. He lifted the cloth on the easel to reveal the painting I had seen in New York of Van Os.

'It is a rich merchant, but a very cantankerous fellow,' said Rembrandt.

'In what ways, dear sir, please tell,' I said, as innocent an ingenue as I could muster.

'Well, he will only let me visit his home at night, and he refuses to pay me in silver, which is awkward, gold is so much harder to transact. Also, I cannot wear my cross or any Christian depiction when I enter his house. He treats his staff poorly, although he is deferential to me. Still, a dark and unhappy household he runs.'

'Is that not the Van Os family that lives on the Herengracht?' I asked.

'Indeed, child, that large house across from the Herengracht Church.'

'I feel you have captured that remarkably well,' I complimented him, ingeniously. 'Pray sir, how do you make this beautiful blue color?—where do you get that from?'

'Madam, an artist should never tell his secrets, but for you, I will make an exception. It's made of lapis lazuli, a rock. It's named ultramarine, or 'beyond the sea', because it originates from a distant land. The color symbolizes holiness and humility; the virgin Mary's robe is usually ultramarine. Nothing humble about the price, though. Miners extract it in Afghanistan, so you can imagine it's very expensive. It is the most expensive color I have, so I use it sparingly. Fortunately for my purse, Amsterdammers are neither holy nor humble. And that damn Vermeer in Delft keeps buying up all the supplies. It works well, especially with his use of it for shading. I'll give him that'

There was a palette on a stool next to the easel, with a dollop of blue on it. I dabbed my finger on the blue that made a small dot. Rembrandt smiled, 'A small present from me to you', he said.

The Zuiderkerk bells rung, as did other church bells, and Rembrandt's eyes lit up. 'It is time, time for the judgement!' he said. 'But we must hurry, or we will miss it.' He threw a beret on his head and grabbed my hand and rushed me outside and along the street, back towards the Dam. Under one arm, he had a sketchbook with loose leaves of paper and a leather pouch containing pencils and crayons and ink nibs.

The mood in the city had changed. Other people were hurrying to the Dam square. A crowd had gathered around the scaffolding, and a young girl was bound to it. She was sobbing uncontrollably, and people were throwing rotten vegetables at her and jeering. A man of law read out the judgement. The crowd was boisterous and agitated, but I could make out that the girl had killed her landlady with a hatchet. They had argued about her late rent payments.

Then, one guard took the same hatchet and hit the girl across the head with it. The crowd cheered. The blow seemed to knock her out, and her head hung to one side. I gasped, horrified. Then a man with a large, plumed hat read out the death sentence, and the guard turned the garrote that was around her neck. The pain of the garrote snapped her out of unconsciousness; she tried to scream, but her throat was constricted. There was a look of pure terror on her face. Horror seized me, and I clasped my hands over my mouth to stifle a cry. I could do nothing to help her. As the crowd watched her life being choked away, silence fell. Finally, thankfully, her head slumped.

There was no celebration. The hushed public slowly left the square, chastened, and the body of the girl was left hanging, her face distorted. Even Rembrandt, who had been trying to sketch the event, had stopped and looked gloomy. The reality and finality of what had just happened had sunk in. Jubilation turned to guilt.

'She was the first female to be executed in twenty years,' he said. 'They will place her body on a stock at the Galgenveld so all sailors entering the port can see how we Amsterdammers deal with lawbreakers.' He seemed to be trying to validate it. Apologetic.

I nodded, trying to hold back the tears. He could see I was upset, so he put his hand on my shoulder and nodded.

The crowd left quickly, and Rembrandt told me to come back soon for his letter to my father and left. I stood looking at the girl, hanging limp on the stock. They would probably leaver her there for a while, as a warning to everybody. I realized I was almost alone with her. I said softly, 'I'm sorry this happened to you', then left as well.

I went to the large house on the Herengracht owned by the Van Os family. It was a 15-minute walk, so I thought about a plan. What would I do? I came up with nothing.

The house was one of the most expensive on the canal, one of the most expensive places in Europe. Curtains draped the windows, highly unusual for the time, and even today. The Dutch culture likes windows to be un-curtained, so everyone can see that nothing improper is going on inside. It was an intimidating building, and this was the lion's den.

I plucked up my courage and pulled the doorbell ringer. I could hear the bell tingle deep in the recesses of the house. Eventually, a rather pale young girl answered the door. She said nothing, she just gazed at me, indifferently.

'I am here to visit the master of the house, Frederik Van Os,' I said.

'And what is the nature of your business?' she asked.

'I am Boudewijna Dol of the Dol family. My husband recently perished in London, and I am now consolidating his business interests. I apologize for turning up uninvited but...' The girl continued to just stare at me, then retreated before I could finish my sentence, closing the door behind her. What was it with the social skills of these people? I waited, but nothing happened.

After I while I pulled the doorbell again, but nothing happened. Eventually, after about ten minutes, just as I was about to leave, the door opened again, and the girl just stood there. I assumed I was being invited in, so I went in. The interior of the building was more lavish than the exterior, which was common in those days. People hid personal wealth from view. It was important not to be ostentatious. Italian marble covered the walls, and a gorgeous chandelier hung in the expansive lobby next to an exquisitely curved French staircase. Portraits on the wall depicted scenes of Greek mythology. Some were bordering on pornographic.

The girl led me, or at least I just followed her, to what seemed like a library. Because the windows were draped, I opened one to let sunlight into the darkroom. The maid rushed over and hurriedly pulled the drape back.

'The master likes the rooms to be dark. He said that the sunlight ruins the books, which are delicate and old.' She lit a few candles, then left. Somehow, I didn't think having candles next to piles of old dried-out books was obviously the smarter solution. I inspected the books.

First editions and expensively bound, in Latin and French, and German. On a pedestal in the middle of the room was the first folio of Shakespeare's works printed in 1623. It was open at Macbeth. On the side table was Sir Isaac Newton's seminal '*Philosophiæ Naturalis Principia Mathematica*'. This was remarkable, as this version of the book would not be published until 1723, fifty odd years in the future. It's strange writing about things in the past that are actually in the present but will occur in the future, but that occurrence in the future is still in the past. Tense can be stressful. However, nothing was surprising to me anymore.

I waited a while. People in the 1660s have no sense of time or urgency, it seems. Eventually, a woman stood at the doorway, at first saying nothing. She startled me.

'Hello', I said. It was dark. I couldn't see her face because she was silhouetted. Her clothes were black, and she had a veil over her face, as if in mourning.

'I am Boudewijna Dol and I am visiting Amsterdam. I am from London. My husband died recently, and I am inquiring about some of his business interests.'

The woman turned and left before I could go any further, neither introducing herself nor acknowledging me. I was being studied and observed.

'Hello Boudewijna Dol' said a man behind me. It was Fredrick Van Os. I hate to admit it, but I did that whooping, panic dance, jazz hands thing again, but got it quickly under control. I composed myself. He was a tall, well-built man, wearing a cape. He had black hair, combed back, and penetrating eyes framed by heavy eyebrows. An intense stare scrutinized me.

'Hello, I am Boudewijna Dol of the Dol family' I said after I had composed myself.

'I know, I just said that,' said the man. 'I am Fredrick Van Os, of the Amsterdam Van Os family. You did a good job finding me so quickly. I hope your journey has not been too troubling. It can be overwhelming for a – newcomer.'

'From London?' I offered, feigning ignorance of what had happened to me.

His eyes narrowed. He was judging me, wondering where to place me. 'No, from New Amsterdam. Sorry, I mean New York, from the future. It's hard to keep track. You would not believe the things I have to keep track of.'

I was glad I didn't have to keep up a pretense, but I knew instinctively I would have to be careful. These people were powerful beyond anything I had experienced, apparently even controlling time.

The pale maid brought in some coffee and some cookies, so we sat at the table. The painting by Rembrandt I had seen was an excellent likeness, so I mentioned that. It pleased him. 'Rembrandt takes his time,' he said, 'but then again, I have all the time in the world.'

'So how does this work? How did you travel through time?' I asked. Van Os looked at me, thinking, deciding something. He looked me up and down, evaluating. Was he deciding to tell me the truth, a lie, a mix, or maybe just kill me and be done with me? There would be no consequences in the future for my death in the far past. The ultimate cold case, dead before I was born. His demeanor was a man who was being patient and indulgent against his character. He was giving me this time because he was a gentleman. He was being kind. Or deciding.

'Well,' he started, as if it was an effort he would rather not start on. 'There have always been these natural portals, mostly in the Northern hemisphere, gateways to different times and places on the Earth. Such portals have always existed, and only stray animals or unfortunate and confused Neanderthals have accidentally used them. It is how homo sapiens reached the Americas.

The foundation poles of Amsterdam, which keep the city from sinking, were unknowingly driven into this anomaly creating an unintended time anchor, allowing time to fold around those who understand its workings. This "portal" is connected to Amsterdam's special location, a delta city built on reclaimed land, where water, trade, and secrecy have always been mixed.

It took a long time, but eventually, a small group of exceptional beings exploited these flaws in the continuum; they understood their value and kept them secret from the rest of the world. This is the elite group of people that your family is, how shall I say it, indirectly associated. The elite guardians employ them and reward them richly.

My family and a few others are Guardians. We prevent abuse of the portals. Where they exist, over the centuries, a metropolis has naturally arisen. There's one in London, Paris, and Amsterdam, of course. New York, as you have experienced. There's one in Siberia but nobody uses that. Rome has one, but has weakened, as they sometimes do.'

'So, you can just travel the past and future and across continents?' I asked, astounded.

'Well, you can only travel to the future if you are in the past. The furthest you can go is the actual future, your future, where you come from, Boudewijna. You cannot go any further. The present is happening at its own pace. But if it's happened, then you can travel back along its timeline. And that is what we do: exploit the knowledge of that trajectory. You could call it an unfair advantage.'

It was the ultimate form of insider trading, I thought, placing bets on races already taken place. Buying shares in future successful companies, shorting the future failures.

I started talking about how interesting that was to me, as a historian, and how much information I could glean from that. He listened, I think, and he took a sip from his coffee and gently dabbed his mouth. Lost in my enthusiasm, I did not notice that he was not really listening. He had decided.

Then, in a flash, he pounced on me like an animal. He grabbed me by the throat with one hand and lifted me up into the air, the ease of which easily betrayed his strength. A mirror behind him showed me hanging in mid-air, my hands grasping and clawing at my throat, his reflection absent from the frame. It was as if his reflection were invisible.

'Listen to me, servant,'—he spat the word servant like it was toxic and bitter in his mouth, 'you are a nobody and I could crush you right now.' His eyes were blazing, his nostrils seemed to flare like a wild animal, and he bared his fangs that had now extended from normal human teeth to large saber-tooth tiger canines. He pushed his face close to mine, snarling. His hot breath washed over my face. I was expecting a blast of sulfur, the odor of putrefying hatred, but his breath was surprisingly minty.

'We can tolerate your snooping into our ancient way of life no more. You are to desist and keep yourself to whatever a small life you have and be deferential to your masters. Do you understand?' I was choking, but tried to nod. I was already feeling faint. That morning's execution of the girl flooded my consciousness, but I needed to focus.

'We will wipe out the Dol family and it's generational wealth if you meddle again in our world.'

He shook me about like a toy doll and then threw me against a wall. I could hardly get up before he grabbed me and threw me again. I felt ribs crack. Pain shot through my body and I cried out. A searing pain, drawing breath, hurt. Instinct told me to make myself small and keep still. He reached out to me again, but the woman had come back and stopped him.

'Stop, Fredrick, it is but a servant. She does not have your strength,' she said. He threw his head back and howled to the gods like a wolf. It was a primeval howl, something that I had never heard before. She grabbed me with one hand by the throat, and carried me, my feet dangling, out into the lobby. I gasped for breath. There was a door that she flung open and it revealed a staircase that led down into the basement. She then hurled me backwards down the stairs. I could see, as I fell backward, Fredrick roaring and the woman framed in the doorway. My heels clipped the steps as I fell backward, my fingers grabbing at the walls, scraping the plaster, finding nothing to hold. The fall seemed to last forever, and I braced myself, waiting to hit the floor at the bottom.

There was a splash, and I landed in deep ink black water. It was cold and dark, and it knocked the breath out of me. Again, a searing pain from my ribs. I tried to hold my breath, but my broken ribs nearly made me scream out in pain. A hand grabbed me, and I tried to fight it off, but it grabbed me again, pulling me upwards. Whoever was grabbing me was in the water as well. I reached the surface and screamed out in pain as the fresh air rushed in and made my chest expand, splintering my ribs even more. A dark sky was above me.

'Keep still, Boudewijna' said a voice. It seemed familiar, and my instincts told me to trust this person. I could see stars above me, lights to one side. The Hudson Bridge. The person pulled me to the bank and dragged me up into the trees. It was Hiro.

'Be quiet, they are searching for you,' he said. We hid in the bushes. Torches from the bridge searched the river bank, but they soon left and it became quiet, only the rhythmic drone of cars hitting the metal road of the bridge as traffic resumed.

The northern tip of Manhattan is surprisingly forested and uninhabited, and it took us a while to walk through the woods to get to the George Washington Bridge, and then find a taxi to take us home. I could walk but was cold, as I had only my underwear and t-shirt on, and the sneakers. The Dutch clothes were gone. The pain from my rib was searing, but fear kept me going.

As we made our way home, a thousand thoughts ran through my head. Back at the flat, I felt a pain in my finger and saw a small splinter still sticking in it, and some brown dirt under one fingernail. I got my sample kit out and retrieved the splinter and the dirt with some tweezers. Was the wood a common Dutch wood sort? Was the dirt nutmeg? There was still a small trace of blue oil paint on my finger, so I sampled that as well.

I showered, to get clean and to warm up, and got dressed. I had torn fingernails and bruises. Hiro and I agreed I would say I slipped on the staircase and Hiro had a private doctor meet us. I had two broken ribs and some bruises. The doctor wrapped me up in gauze to support my rib and gave me some painkillers. He assessed there was no internal bleeding, but should get an x-ray as soon as possible to be sure. My side looked black and blue from the bruising.

After the doctor left, Hiro and I discussed what had happened. He had returned to the flat as he wanted to discuss some details about Amsterdam when he saw I was being bundled into the car, and he had followed on his motorbike. This was probably not true on his part. Hiro was just being the diligent bodyguard. He was probably just waiting for me to get safely home. He never liked me thinking he was stalking me, and he was right to think so. However, if he had been elsewhere perfecting his sushi, while I was being kidnapped and thrown off a bridge, that wouldn't have been good either.

Hiro told me the police cars blocked his view, but he saw what looked like me going over the side. He said it took him a good ten minutes to get down the side of the riverbank to the river. He just dived in and was lucky to find me. I told him I couldn't remember anything. Which was partially true.

Hiro and I reviewed theories of what had just occurred, and I suggested that someone in my family had been doing something that had displeased someone, and maybe this was a warning or a threat or a message. I did not tell Hiro about what had really happened, or what I had seen.

We agreed we would keep the New York police out of it, that I would investigate on my own. As I was leaving for Amsterdam the next day, it would be safer. Eventually, after we spent an hour lying to each other, Hiro retired to the spare bedroom, and I went and sat at the window. I looked out at the Manhattan skyline. Despite its immensity, it was strangely calming.

An email arrived on my phone. It was from the Port Authority Police Department. They informed me that my request for CTV files from the Henry Hudson Bridge had been approved and that I could download the requested file via a hyperlink. This was strange. I had requested nothing from the Port Authority, and even if I had, my experience as an Amsterdam Police Detective leads me to believe my request would not have been approved so quickly. I clicked the link, and it downloaded a large video file.

It was a video of me on the bridge, but I was just standing there. I was smoking a cigarette for about 5 minutes, pacing up and down at the apex of the bridge. That is not what happened. I have not smoked in years. The two police officers approach me, slowly. I throw the cigarette and then jump over the side of the bridge. The officers run to catch me, but they are too late. This was not what happened, but this is what the CTV cameras were showing. They had doctored it, and spared no expense. It must be A.I.

A second email arrived from an anonymous email account. It was my medical files, stating that I had a history of depression, and I take prescription drugs that sometimes have the side effects of hallucinations if taken them too regularly, or too much. Nothing else was in the email, nothing else needed to be.

These 'guardians' don't play around. The video was so convincing, and the report so damning, that I even doubted myself. This was a warning. Backdown, stay away, I was out of my league. This is how they handled my father, and now I understand why he was terrified. He feared for his family and for us.

The next day, I flew back to Amsterdam. As I watched Boston pass by and as the Canadian wilderness merges into the mountainous backbone of Greenland, I tried to focus on my next steps. The so-called guardians just wanted me to go away. Could I do that? Would they leave me alone if I did that? Every bump in turbulence hurt my ribs, but the painkillers were kicking in.

What did I want to do? And if I wanted to do something, how was I going to do it? Overwhelmed and exhausted emotionally from the last few days, I drifted off to sleep. The hard bounce of the plane landing at Schiphol in Amsterdam woke me up. The pain of my ribs flooded back.

Chapter 5

If you don't believe in time travel, you have just done it. As you idly turned the page, six weeks have passed for me. I had lain low to regroup. Perhaps it was an emotional response to the danger faced by me and my family. It was not something I could take lightly. I went to the police station straight from the airport and immediately started work on a gigantic pile of administrative work on my desk that needed to be taken care of. I used the pile of folders and boxes to hide from my colleagues.

My ribs still hurt, I could not sleep on my left side, and it hurt to breathe. My breathing became shallower, and that was tiring me. I had some bruises, but no dizziness or nausea, suggesting no internal bleeding. Another doctor's visit confirmed it. It would take six weeks to heal, he said.

He offered me more painkillers, but I declined. I liked the pain. It reminded me, like a souvenir, of what had happened. My cracked rib was a painful reminder that what I'd been through was real, not some figment of my imagination. It happened; it was real, no matter how crazy. But maybe it was a dream, injuries from the effects of the fall?

I assumed I was being watched, so everything I did was to present a chastened and obliging servant to the outside world. My emails were social and about anything and everything except my mystical experience and what had happened at the Van Os house. I was upbeat, and seemingly just getting on with my life after having my wrist slapped by the 'Guardians'. I played that role.

Hiro was in Japan for a visit. He left reluctantly, but I insisted. I knew I was safe as long as l kept a low profile.

My home security system texted me during work. There was an intruder in my apartment. I checked the security cameras, and there was a man sitting in the chair near the window overlooking the canal. He had his feet up on the windowsill and was calmly reading a book. The light from the window silhouetted him, so I could not see his face. I reviewed footage from other cameras; he was alone. There was nobody there, or outside in the hallway. My front door camera showed no damage, so someone had expertly picked my high-range locks. This told me that this man knew what he was doing and therefore knew that I could see him and knew that he was there.

I left work and went home. I checked the cars near my flat for anyone waiting to ambush me, but they were all empty. No one was around. Hiro was frantically calling on my phone. He had received the same security email, so I tried to calm him down. I told him not to worry and that I would be extra careful. He was not happy and swore profusely in Japanese. I felt reassured that I had my police gun with me and was wearing my uniform. I checked the hallway, slowly moving from one blind spot in the hall to the next, but I was alone. My heart pounded in my rib-cage, throbs of pain from my injuries distracted me from my fear.

The staircase to the third floor, an oak wood, elegant spiral with marble walls, was empty. Suddenly, the kids from the neighbors opened their door and ran out. My hand that was placed on the revolver twitched, but they ran noisily past me, clanging their skateboards on the stone steps as they left for the Vondel Park. I checked the security camera on my phone. He was still sitting in the same chair, although scrubbing through the footage I could see he occasionally got up to get something to drink or stretch his legs.

As I had guessed, no one had forced the front door; it remained unlocked and ajar. This told me that whoever was in there was warning me he was in there. He was expecting me. I opened the door slowly, and it creaked. I pulled out my gun then entered the room. The hallway was empty, but I checked everything. Behind the door, anyplace someone else could be lurking. The room I had seen him in my camera was to the right. I slowly turned the corner, pistol ready to confront whoever it was who had intruded in my private space.

'Ok, keep your hands where I can see them,' I said.

'Oh, hello Bou, you're home early.' It was my cousin, Vincent.

'Vincent, what are you doing? Why did you break into my flat? Why didn't you call me?'

'Well, as you had given me a key and told me I could crash whenever I want, I thought it was okay. Also, I didn't want to disturb you at work.'

'True,' I admitted, holstering my gun. I felt shaken, but I tried to calm myself down.

'You have a gun—wow,' he said. 'I've bought some groceries—I'd thought I could make my famous Spaghetti Bolognese if you like. And some wine. I also bought a little present for you.' It was a white noise machine.

I was still a little rattled, so I poured myself a drink. Vincent took out the white noise machine and put it next to a lamp. He seemed very pleased with it, cycling through the different options of "Ocean Wave" and "Rain Forest." I smiled and tried to compose myself. He turned on the pure white noise and then said, 'Looks like you have been playing with vampires.' His words shocked me. How did he know?

He put his finger to his mouth to tell me to be quiet. He came over to me and whispered in my ear.

'There is a wiretap in the apartment. They are listening to us. The white noise machine is blocking it. They can hear what we are saying in the kitchen, but not near the white noise machine or over by the window. When I turn the machine off, you tell me you like it, especially the Rain Forest, so I will turn it back on again. We will have a pleasant conversation over dinner in the Kitchen then we will play scrabble by the window, and then I will tell all.'

We cooked together and talked about our families and caught up. I tried not to rush my food, but we soon wandered over to the window to play scrabble. Vincent poured us some wine. I texted Hiro to put him out of his misery and he responded immediately even though it was 4 am.

'Assume two things,' Vincent said. 'They are watching us, tapping into your security cameras, and that I will win, as I am very good at scrabble.'

We set up the scrabble board, and I told Vincent everything that had happened. He nodded and smiled and gave the occasional comment. However, he remained unshocked and unsurprised. He occasionally put down a scrabble word that was relevant and sometimes profane.

'So, am I crazy?' I asked. 'Did this happen?'

'You are not, and it did. The Guardians have been around for centuries, and we Servants – you, me, your family, and hundreds of families around the world, have served them.

The Guardians are eight families making up the Syndicate. The Van Os family is one. They are very enigmatic, they have incredible wealth, but because they are few, they need help, and they depend on the servant's families. It's a fragile balance. Most of the servants are only vaguely aware of the actual nature of the Guardians. Your father found out when dealing with the problems around your sister'

'Someone raped her; that wasn't just "a problem",' I hissed, surprising myself.

'My apologies. I was just being careful. The Guardians need the servants. It's a house of cards. That's why you are safe. For now. You have received a warning, but if you cause trouble, the guardians and the servants will feel threatened and may align themselves against you. It has happened before. The Dol family wealth, impressive as it is, will not help you.'

'Tell me everything you know,' I said. 'Hide nothing. Start at the beginning.'

Vincent went to the kitchen and poured himself another drink. He chatted about the parties he had been to and the places he had been. He acted a little drunk, all show for the cameras and for anyone listening in. Then he settled back in his chair by the window, making himself comfortable.

'The masters have access to a natural phenomenon that occurs within the earth, a time portal that has its entrance in one place and an exit at the other. A western portal always goes to the present time. The eastern portal goes back in time but changes on a calendar that is complicated and affected by the moon, solar pulses, the position of the planets. Universal things. There are several portals throughout the world, and major cities have sprouted up around them. The masters have figured it out, and use that to their advantage. It's not entirely accurate, a solar flare can change the time by ten years. That's why the masters use servants to test things out. The portal changes a traveler's DNA. Once you have been though the portal, you need to return occasionally to rejuvenate. If you don't, you suddenly desiccate. I think you have seen some examples. The masters have travelled over centuries, but the effects are that they become incredibly light sensitive, so prefer the dark as much as possible. They are very strong, but have surprising weaknesses. I've heard they don't like a certain smells or colors, and are obsessed with their standing within the masters social hierarchy. They are probably the inspiration of the vampire legends, but this is all I know.'

'They drink blood?' I asked.

Vincent smiled. 'Maybe, but they are of another species. I'm not sure if it's because the DNA has changed or they have evolved naturally. Or have paid for their enhancements'.

We sat in silence for a while.

'They are also incredibly arrogant, and so used to getting their own way without consequences. Take Oetgens for example. He uses human ash from exceptional people to create his own 'terroir' experiments for his grapes. Madness.'

'The Guardians had been around for a while, traveling back in time to influence politics to their advantage. Mostly bribing and cajoling, with the occasional assassination. They meddled in the senate in Rome and manipulated things throughout Egypt and Asia. There is a portal in a pyramid. They came occasionally to Amsterdam, which was little more than a swamp that connected Germany to the North Sea. The Van Os family controlled the portal, quietly influencing affairs and managing the servants.'

'But then, in 1595, a rather incompetent sailor called De Houtman took a ship and sailed from Amsterdam to Indonesia to trade in spices. All thought that the Portuguese and others would block him, but despite his bungling, he still did some trade and came back alive. It proved something that was thought not possible. Trade in the far countries without meddling from the Portuguese. Investors in Amsterdam thought they could do better and sent another ship with a much more competent crew.'

'They were incredibly successful, and the profits from the investment in the trade were often astronomical. Soon, fleets made their way to the far east. Primitive navigation and piracy made seafaring highly speculative. To cover those risks, as no investor would want to place all his wealth on one ship, shares spread the cost and risks over several ships and investors. If you bought the right shares, and the right insurance policies, with insider knowledge, with knowledge from the future about the past, you could make inconceivable wealth.'

I watched Vincent's jaw tighten as he spoke, his voice low and deliberate. His usual amiable smile was gone, replaced by a weight that settled in his eyes. He leaned forward, his fingers laced together, his knuckles white. The air between us felt heavier, charged with something unspoken.

'I need you to listen,' he said, his tone measured, unwavering.

I swallowed, my pulse quickening. Whatever this was, it wasn't a joke.

'The Guardians saw this as a perfect opportunity to accumulate wealth and power. The Van Os family were the gatekeepers to the Amsterdam portal. Quick to recognize the potential, they used their inside information to manipulate the system.'

Vincent paused and took a sip from his glass. 'In 1602, they formed the world's first multinational corporation, the Dutch East India Company.'

Vincent took some scrabble tiles from the bag and arranged the letters to form the word 'stocks'.

'They didn't just stop at trading spices. They had their hands in everything - tea, cotton, silks. And with their influence stretching centuries into the future, they had intimate knowledge of market trends before they even happened.'

His eyes met mine solemnly as he continued, 'This, of course, meant that they could manipulate not just their own fortunes but those of entire countries and economies. It was a blatant abuse of power.'

'And their influence didn't stop in Amsterdam. They spread their tentacles across to the New World, in New York and elsewhere', Vincent continued, his fingers dancing over the Scrabble tiles before placing 'empire' on the board. 'Everywhere they went, they manipulated economies and markets for their own benefit.'

He paused momentarily, running his hand through his thick tousled hair. A look of weary resignation etched onto his features. 'I'm telling you this because I don't want to see you get hurt, Boudewijna. They have their eyes on you now, and you need to tread carefully.'

His words were a chilling warning, a stark reminder of the dangerous game I was playing. I took another sip of my wine, feeling its warmth slowly unfurl within me as I processed his revelations.

'So, what's the solution?' I asked.

Vincent shrugged helplessly. 'They've been around for centuries, Bou. Their power is deeply entrenched. Promise me you will keep away from them. They are vicious.'

'They are so unbelievably wealthy that money means nothing to them. What is important to them is their privacy, and their social standing within the tribes. The Van Os family are very protective of their portal. The tribes collaborate occasionally but usually keep to themselves.

But something is up. The Amsterdam portal is transitioning through the 1600s to when the first stocks and shares were created. I think the Van Os family is making a power move. Or maybe another clan is attempting to take over the Van Os family wealth at the source. You can feel the tribes swarming.'

We sat for a while in silence. 'Let's go for a walk', he said, and I nodded. We went outside and walked for a while in silence. We walked to the end of the Herengracht and turned right to walk along the Amstel. The river was busy with small pleasure craft and tourist boats. I stopped before one house near the corner with a plain gray stone facade. Locals knew it as the 'House with the Blood Stains'. On its facade were marks with strange reddish-brown symbols. These were said to be the blood of a man who once lived in the house. Coenraad Van Beuningen was a six-time mayor of Amsterdam and a successful ambassador. Despite all his political achievements and social status, van Beuningen lost a fortune in speculation, and went mad.

Supposedly, one night, in a fit of frenzy, Van Beuningen leaped through his bedroom window after being confined for his protection.

The broken glass caused him to bleed; he calmly used his blood to make the drawings until they took him away. Van Beuningen painted arcane cabalistic signs on the gray stone of his building. Strange symbols and images of the masted sail ships were discernable.

I pointed them out to Vincent. I had already taken photographs, previously, to study later. But it seemed to resonate with us now, considering the time travel we were talking about.

'Maybe it's not the best way to send messages across the centuries', said Vincent. I agreed.

We walked further.

'Who was the woman that saved you, who sent you back through the portal?' he asked.

'You mean the woman who threw me down a flight of stairs?' I responded. I didn't know, but then remembered the lady who had lectured me in New York. Was that her? She was a Van Os. I told Vincent, and he nodded. 'Sounds right'.

We walked back to my flat. We acted as normally as we could, finishing our game of scrabble, and then I helped Vincent make up the spare bed. The next day, when I got up, Vincent had already left. There was a note on the kitchen island.

'Be safe Bou. I will contact you soon.'

I went to the Station and worked on more cases. I wanted to lose myself in my work. An anonymous email with a picture attachment arrived at my workplace in the afternoon. It was Vincent and me walking along the canal. Nothing else was in the email. It was a message. I know that if they wanted something to happen to me, it would have happened already. It was a warning. But did this mean that Vincent was in trouble as well?

I decided not to reach out to him. He would appear again soon enough, and reaching out to him might create unnecessary attention. I wanted to protect him. He was right; they were too powerful, too rich. I may not like it, but I had to take off myself. So I worked on my cases, and time passed. But after about two weeks, with no response from Vincent, I sent him an email.

'Hi Cous. What's up? Are you in Amsterdam soon? Let's play scrabble again!' I did not get a reply, which was not unusual for Vincent.

A few days later, I was out walking and passed the "House with the Blood Stains". Was it just a coincidence, or did I subconsciously walk by? I pulled the text message I sent Vincent. I stared at my phone, my thumb hovering over the screen. The last message sat unread, its timestamp growing older by the day. I bit my lip, resisting the urge to send another. Vincent always replied, if not after a while, but always in the end. I tapped the edge of the phone against my palm, a tight knot forming in my stomach. Should I text again? Would that bring unwanted attention from the Guardians?

Then I noticed something on the grey stone facade of the building. Down in the left-hand corner were three letters, barely discernable. They were different as they were not red or ochre like the other markings, but in a faded blue. I had not seen them before. Had I not noticed them, or were they new? I took a photo with my phone and then went directly home.

I compared the photos with the photos I had in my archive. I was right; The marking was new, and yet it seemed timeworn and faded. I opened the picture of the blue markings in Photoshop. The blue had faded, but there was also an indentation, as if the person who had made the marks had used a sharp implement to groove the letters. I separated out the colors and increased the contrast. Smoke and pollution covered these grooves over the years, but I could make out the basic shape. It was the letters BOU. Could Vincent have made these marks? Did they send Vincent back into the past, as they sent me?

I touched the photo on the screen. I could almost feel the groves of the letters BOU on my fingertips. My pulse hammered in my ears. A cold, creeping sensation crawled up my spine. The room suddenly felt smaller, the walls pressing in. My stomach twisted. If Vincent was now there in the past... then everything he had told me was true.

A tiny, vibrant dot caught my attention. Using Photoshop, I sampled the color of a blue pixel. The color was ultramarine. Yet another color to add to my rainbow of evidence.

Hiro came back that night. It was good to see him. He was my rock. I spent the next few days trying to figure things out. I needed more information and decided, hesitantly, to go to France to visit my family. Theo and Thea would be there.

The moment I stepped off the train, the scent of fresh bread and damp cobblestones wrapped around me like an old embrace. The chatter of rural French filled the air, warm and familiar, settling deep in my chest. My father would pick me up at the train station. I exhaled slowly, the tension I had been carrying finally loosening. Home.

A burst of laughter echoed from the cafe on the corner—the same cafe where my father used to bring me for chocolat chaud on rainy afternoons. Father arrived in his car, so I suggested we have a chocolat in the cafe for old times' sake. He looked a few years older. He had retired now and was oil painting to keep himself busy. A carefree life, in a carefree place. I wondered if I should disturb his peace with my problems.

After, when we got home, it was heartening to feel my childhood memories flooding back. A memory of normality. Inside the house, the wooden floor creaked just as it always had. My mother's voice called from the kitchen, with the maids fussing around her. The scent of simmering herbs filled the air. For the first time in a long time, I felt safe.

After a delicious meal, I settled in the library with my father to play chess. We sipped cognac, and I told him about the cases I had been working on. It seemed prudent to keep my latest adventure to the last. I wanted to see how he was reacting to my stories. I told him about the desiccated mummies. That seemed a good way to broach the subject.

I could see him stiffen slightly, so I knew he knew what I was talking about.

'I know about the Guardians' I said, finally. He sat quietly, staring at a chess piece in his hand, turning it around and around, lost in thought. 'Stay away from those people, Bou.' he said. 'How much do you know?' I asked. 'Enough to know they can destroy us, our family, our future generations'.

'And our ancestors', I added. There, I had said it. My father just looked at me. He looked weary. My father has the envious habit of thinking before he speaks, which sometimes leads to pauses in the conversation. Most people fill that void with more talk, but I know my father well, and I let him think. He sat back in his chair. The fire crackled. With a single gulp, he emptied his cognac glass. Glass in his hand reflected the flames from the fire. He was deep in thought.

'Our family went through a terrible period, with what happened to Thea. It was the worst time of my life. I had to make hard decisions. Decisions that I did not want to make but I had to protect my family, future and past generations. I don't want to go through that again.'

'You can't let these people dominate you like this,' I said.

'Do you know how I met your mother?' he asked.

'Of course, at a party at the Hamptons', I said. I was an old family story.

'What if I had not gone to that party? What if a business meeting has stopped me, or a missed train connection? Or food poisoning. Do you know how easy it is to disrupt the flow of time? The Dol family has made its fortunes mostly honestly, but there have been times, in the past, when insider knowledge has helped the business move forward.'

'Who cares about money,' I said, as only a wealthy person could hypothesize.

'Everything about what we have is a random weave of circumstance and coincidence. When we had the trouble with Thea, the problem could have been solved by something happening the night your mother and I conceived Thea and Theo. Then they would not exist. We would be ignorant of them. We would follow this path of fate in ignorance. They could have done that. They do that. I had to make sure I protected Theo and Thea. I needed to protect the entire family.'

'So why didn't they do that? Why don't they go back in time and stop you meeting Mum, or Grandpa Dol meeting Grandma Dol, or whatever?'.

'Because it became too disruptive, the shockwaves of time had too many consequences. It happens outside the Guardians and Servants, but inside our families, it's done as a last resort. I had to contain the damage. The Guardian elders are very protective of the disruptions in time. Let the past be the past Bou.'

I thought for a while, assuming my father's habit. Then I said, 'Vincent is gone'.

Father sighed, 'Yes, well we all love Vincent, but he comes and goes as he wishes.' He didn't convince me, but I knew I could not concern my father with my worries. I promised him I was going to keep a low profile, I would not cause trouble.

The next day, I went truffle hunting with our truffle dog, Peppa IIV, who was not a pig. Long story. Theo and Thea took me into the forest, the hundred acres we owned that surrounded our Chateau. We walked along a path I had often walked as a child. They had found some black truffles, it was the season, and we were hopeful of finding more. It was always strange to see Theo and Thea as adults in this wood where we had played so often as children. Thea was then always the high spirited one, always running ahead, a mother or grandmother of Peppa (also called Peppa), yapping at her ankles.

Now it was Theo who was marching ahead, calling for the dog, hitting the undergrowth with his stick. He had grown; his new wife pregnant, successful within the Dol family enterprise as an investment banker. Thea was different, often staying at the Chateau. She seemed to be stuck, in inertia.

'How is Amsterdam?' asked Thea as we walked along the path. 'I should come visit again sometime; I always love Amsterdam. I'm getting lazy in my old age'.

'You are always welcome, Thea.' I said. When Theo was sufficiently far ahead, I had slowed our walk to a slow pace, I told Thea about Vincent.

'Really? Are you concerned? Vincent is always off somewhere doing Vincent things'.

'This is just between you and me,' I said, looking ahead at Theo.

'My, you are being mysterious', said Thea.

'I think Vincent has gotten in with the wrong people somehow. They might be the same people from that party, you know, the one with the trouble.' I didn't need to say anything more. Thea's faced dropped, and she started walking.

'I have put that all behind me Bou, it's not something I think about anymore. There are things that you don't understand. I need to protect Father and the family.' I nodded. I told her what I knew. My knowledge, and that of others, surprised and saddened her.

We walked a little in silence. 'I need to make sure Vincent is safe. Is there anything you can tell me about that night, the people, anything you remember.'

Theo emerged from the forest further up the path, holding up what looked like a truffle. 'I found one' he shouted. The dog barked around his feet.

Thea spoke, quietly, quickly. 'I was drugged, I don't remember much. But what happened was not just about sexual assault, it was a power play. It was a statement by Guardians, or a specific guardian, a power play over the servants. The crime went further than just between the raper and his victim.'

'What do you remember about the raper - did you know him?'

'I could never identify him, but I sure he was from the Van Os family. They were there that night, and unusually rowdy, like it was some sort of full moon.'

Theo became occupied with some undergrowth as we neared him. Then he went into the forest again, chasing the dog. Thea turned to face me. 'All I remember is he was unusually strong. I remember a strong smell, like Japanese peppermint, and a roar, a primeval roar, like a mix between a wolf and a lion.'

She turned and ran off after Theo. I knew she would not or could not tell me anything more; she was ending the conversation. But she had told me enough.

A few days later, I returned to Amsterdam.

Chapter 6

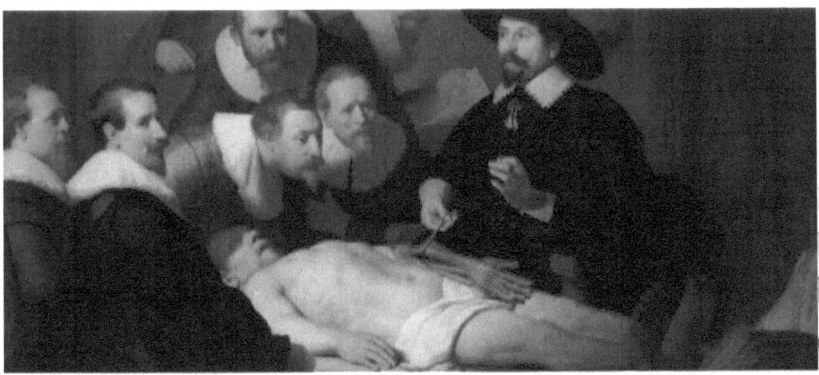

Back in Amsterdam, I did as much research as I could. Using a burner phone, I texted Vincent repeatedly but received no reply. I looked through old documents from the time, and at paintings, especially by Rembrandt. I was intrigued by '*The Anatomy Lesson of Dr. Nicolaes Tulp*' which showed the dissection of a convicted criminal. Sprawled across the table lay the dead man; his pale body, hand, and arm extended, broken and lifeless. The sinews in his arm and hand exposed. Surrounding him, watchful, absorbed, indifferent faces studied his exposed flesh as if he were merely an object. The people in the painting wore clothes similar to those I'd seen on the streets, even though Rembrandt had already painted it before I was there. There was the stillness to the corpse. Rembrandt depicted him as an object of observation and study, dissecting his existence before indifferent men.

A strange, familiar weight settled inside me, cold and heavy. Did I feel like him? Stripped down, laid bare, reduced to something for others to examine?

I exhaled slowly, forcing myself to look away. But even as I turned, the dead man's empty gaze seemed to follow me. In an ink drawing, a pilloried, executed body of a girl hung limply. I had witnessed her death. Rembrandt had drawn her a few days later when her body was hanging at the Galgenveld. Staring at the limp body hanging on the pillory, her sad face in tormented sleep, it made me sad for Vincent. Was he now there, in that place of quick deaths and dissections? I felt my Delft Blauw cat coming back, a sinking feeling in the pit of my stomach. But my depression was based on frustration, a melancholy acceptance of what was wrong with the world. Should I give up? I looked at the face of Elsje in the drawing. Her life was over. Her body, long gone now, was turning to dust. Could Vincent end up there, framed a murderer?

I had tests done on the samples I had taken. The red dot was indeed blood. The two blue dots were ultramarine paint, made from Lapis Lazuli with linseed oil, not synthetic ultramarine. The dirt was a mix of Dutch clay soil and human ash. The splinter was 17th century wood, with traces of nutmeg. It all added up, or at least nothing disproved my worst fears.

I decided I had to find out more, even if that meant it was a threat to me and my family. It was time to take action. I did more research, tried out some connections, but for all intents and purposes, I kept a low profile.

Some weeks afterward, I traveled to New York. Flying west to New Amsterdam on a later flight, I watched the lights of Amsterdam's horseshoe shape fade below.

In New York, I tried to do more research. Then I saw that there another meeting of the Dutch Society, so I attended. I had no actual plan. I would see what would happen, how people would react to me.

I just turned up. Although everyone was friendly, a palpable tension lingered among some attendees. I saw Pieter Oetgens, the owner of the Manhattan vineyard, and he ignored me. I drifted around, chatting, switching to English, then back to Dutch. It all seemed so polite. Just as I was getting bored, the woman I'd spoken with at the previous meeting showed up next to me. She startled me.

'Welcome back, Boudewijna.' she said. 'Hello again,' I said. 'I don't think we have formally met?'

'Lizbeth Van Os, of the Van Os family. You may have heard of us. We have met before, a long, long time ago.'

'I think we have a mutual, er, friend, we met while I was in Amsterdam.' I asked.

'Ah, yes, that was my step-brother.' She just looked at me for a while, thinking. Assessing me, like a teacher would a child. I asked her about her stay in New York but she did not answer, just kept appraising me, looking me up and down. I chatted again, but she was not listening, and just cut me off, as if I could have nothing possibly interesting to say to her.

'I would be careful. Boudewijna.' She said my name as if it tasted weird, like she was a strict teacher at an elementary school, speaking to a silly child.

'There are things at play that you have no knowledge or concern with. It is the changing season for our families. Of course you don't know what that means, but it is an important time for...' and here she paused to think of the right word, 'for our type. Not just the Van Os, but several powerful families who are very influential.'

'Of course, I understand I need to be discrete.' Then I paused, as if to broach another subject, totally unrelated to our conversation. 'I am worried about Vincent, my cousin.' I had to ask. She just looked at me.

'Now is not the time,' she said. Not as advice, but as a statement. Then she walked off, uninterested in my response, looking for something to amuse her. The conversation was over. I was of no longer interest to her.

The crowd was polite, but I noticed some people were consciously avoiding me, moving away when I entered their space. It was getting too frustrating, so I left.

I sat by the window in my New York flat, looking out at the Manhattan skyline. It never failed to impress me, the juxtaposition of the tall monolithic buildings compared to the small cute sixteenth century houses balanced on tree trunks in the swamp that is Amsterdam.

The Empire state building, lit up red and blue. The Freedom Tower. Busy streets below, filled with people and cars, and noisy garbage trucks. The city stretched before me, a sea of lights flickering against the dark. Skyscrapers stood like silent sentinels, their glass facades reflecting the pulse of a city that never sleeps.

From up here, everything was smaller. The honking taxis, the hurried crowds, the millions of untold stories woven through the streets. My story, too, was just one of many. Yet at this moment, I felt finite. Lost in the city's hum, in a place filled with millions of people, I had never felt so alone.

The next day I was walking around the west village, trying to distract myself. I needed to calm my head so I could get my thoughts together. As I meandered through the quaint, tree-lined streets of the West Village, the familiar charm of historic brownstones and cobblestone pathways offered little solace. The neighborhood's vibrant cafes and boutiques, a source of comfort, now seemed to underscore my profound sense of frustration and loss. Each corner I turned reminded me of moments shared with Vincent, making the bustling energy of the city feel paradoxically isolating.

The weight of my grief was palpable, casting a shadow over the picturesque surroundings. Passing by the Hudson River Park, where we once spent carefree afternoons, I felt an overwhelming surge of emotion. The bohemian spirit of the West Village, with its bohemian vibe, made me grapple with the memories and confront the void left behind.

I passed a quaint jewelry store with handmade trinkets and other frivolous things. It made me feel sad. Artisans crafted them to express beauty and joy, yet I felt sadness instead. The jewelry sparkled under the soft glow of the display lights, each delicate piece a testament to patience and precision. Gold filigree twisted into impossibly intricate patterns, gemstones set so perfectly they looked like they belonged there, like they had been nowhere else.

I pressed my fingers lightly against the cool glass, exhaling softly. Someone had poured hours, days—maybe even years—into perfecting these pieces, each carefully cut, each polished surface reflecting a life's work. Purpose. Dedication.

My reflection hovered between the shimmering necklaces, faint and ghostlike. In the middle of the window was a rack holding about ten necklaces and rosaries, all made of small blue stones. Lapis Lazuli, ultramarine, from Afghanistan. What was it that Rembrandt said? That Ultramarine was expensive? Ultramarine represented holiness and humility? Nobody that he knew in Amsterdam. I knew ultramarine had a meaning, that Vincent might have been trying to communicate that.

I then suddenly knew what I had to do. I bought as many of the lapis lazuli bracelets and necklaces as I could, with some gold and silver trinkets, then went back to my apartment.

That night, I packed a small backpack with some stuff I thought might be handy, placing all my jewellery into a cloth bag. At the bottom of the backpack I saw a pack of cigarettes, and I thought, why not? Let's take those as well.

I knew there was a time portal in the East River. I had travelled it. The guardians had already threatned my family by their treatment of my sister. Now they had taken Vincent. Would they just whittle away at everything I held dear till there was nothing left? I could not abandon Vincent.

I took a taxi up to Spuyten Duyvil, where the Hudson Bridge spans the East river from Manhattan to the Bronx. After the taxi left, I walked back across the bridge to where this story began. My plan was to jump off, jump back in time, to find Vincent. But looking over the edge into the cold, dark waters below brought me to my senses. What if it didn't work, or didn't work the way I hoped? My nerves were getting the better of me, so I pulled out a cigarette and lit it. I paced back and forth, looking over the side, then taking another drag of my cigarette.

Someone must have called the police, because a police car pulled up and two cops jumped out. They were not the same police as the previous time, and they approached me carefully, shouting at me to stay away from the edge. I knew it was now or never. I ran to the edge, stared at the cold black water swirling below me. The horn of a passing Amtrak train overwhelmed the police officers' calls. They ran towards me. Was I jumping back in time, or maybe even jumping to my death? I closed my eyes and then stepped out.

As I fell, I realized that the scene that had just played out was exactly the same as the video that they had sent me after my first trip back in time. What I thought was a fake recreation, was actually from the future. Or was it just coincidence? Fear rushed in. Was I making the right decision? It was colder than the last time. I could feel the cold air rush past me. I tried to get my body into the right position for the hitting the water, feet first, leaning back. Was I better prepared this time? Was this the right spot? What if I needed to hit a certain mark? It seemed more silent this time. Was it because I wasn't screaming? Did I need to do anything else? I thought of Thea and Vincent and my family. Maybe I would die. Maybe this was it.

Last time I was hurtling down towards the Hudson River, I thought of revenge. I thought about that again. It's funny how much you can think about in 2.5 seconds.

Splash.

The last time I had felt the wetness and cold, but I had felt tired, so tired, and had drifted off into sleep. Now, the speed of my descent had dragged me down deep into the black waters. I felt disoriented. I didn't know what was up or down. Maybe this was not going to work. I panicked and tried to get back to the surface, but which way was up? The water was murky. A current seemed to drag me down. Or was it up? Should I swim against it or let it carry me up? I felt

an overwhelming urge to breathe, but I could not let the water into
my lungs. The urge grew greater. Air escaped from my mouth and
went downwards. That was where the surface must be. Bubbles do
not sink. I chased the bubbles, but consciousness started to leave me.
Where was the surface? Why was I so deep in the water? Why is this
taking so long? Blackness closed in on me. Blackness of the water,
then a blackness in my mind, like a quietness, a peace. Nothing existed
anymore, nothing was relevant. Nothing was important. A sense that
it was my struggles to reach the surface which was bringing me danger.
Serenity and calm should be my approach. Inertia would keep me
safe. I stopped swimming and just hung suspended in the water. All
movement, everything, was gone. Just let me sleep for a little bit, then I
will sort it out.

Cold turned to a warmness. A feeling of floating turned to the
weight of my body on soft sheets. The smell of nutmeg surrounded me.
Light returned, first random shafts, dust reflected in the rays. There
were some noises. Was that children playing? I was so tired. So tired. I
turned on my side. Just let me sleep a few more minutes. I need to rest.

'Get up' said a woman's voice, irritated and impatient. I could guess
who it was.

I looked around. I was in the same bedstee as the previous time. The
curtains of the bedstee were closed. I rubbed my eyes. 'Just a minute'
I said. That I could not sleep longer irritated me. The awareness that I
was still alive did not even occur to me.

'Now', said the voice. The realization of where I was and what had
happened drifted back into my consciousness.

I pushed open the bedstee doors and saw Lizbeth Van Os, standing
there, arms crossed. She was not pleased.

'You are a stubborn one.' she spat. It was not a compliment. I
climbed out of the bedstee and I walked unsteadily over to the window.
Outside, sixteenth century Amsterdam was busily working its day, just

as before. Street sellers, beggars, chickens pecked by the canal. The smell of sewage filled my nostrils.

'We know you are here, and here you will stay.' she said.

'Keep out of trouble, or your family will face the consequences.' she warned. She meant it. Then left. This was a woman who did not like to chit-chat.

All I wanted to do was sleep, so I got back into the bedstee and lay there, staring at the wooden ceiling. I needed to find Vincent. But where to start? Where in sixteenth century Amsterdam could he be? I looked at the room. There was a chair with some clothes hanging on it. A petticoat, a house gown and a collar. On the chair was a plate with bread and cheese and slices of apple. I checked out the clothes. I wanted to look as inconspicuous as possible. Drained, I dressed slowly, then ate some food. It was delicious, even for simple fare, and I felt my energy returning. There was a knock on the door, and a young man walked in.

'Hello, Boudewijna, my name is Kees Van Haverman', he said. It was the same person who had met me when I travelled back in time, but he looked much younger. 'What year is this?' I asked. He didn't seem surprised I asked. It must be a question he gets asked a lot.

'1639', he said.

My last visit was in 1664, the year they executed that girl in Dam square. Now I had gone further back in time. Hanging on the chair, hidden first under the clothes, was my backpack. Inside were still the necklaces and trinkets. I stuffed them into my petticoat pockets. I made my excuses and made my way out to the Amsterdam streets.

There were fewer buildings on the canal belt, but there was still the same hustle and bustle. There seemed to be more foreigners. A man walks past me, wearing fine clothes. He had a large molensteenkraag, or collar, and other fineries that let everyone know he was affluent. Strangely, a young boy servant followed behind him, holding up a cushion on what rested was a tulip bulb.

I wandered the streets, first going to the Dam square, then walking towards the docks. On the bridge that crossed the Amstel, close to where the future Central Station would be built, was a small wooden shed. A group of people stood around the hut waving small pieces of paper. They were trying to buy or sell shares in ships that were trading spices.

A young man, with a forced smile, desperate, came to me and asked me if I wanted to buy shares from him. He was wearing a doublet of wool and silk, trimmed with subtle embroidery, but I could see it was a little worn and had seen better days. The gentlemen there all wore smart, yet understated, clothing, subtly balancing modest Calvinist values and the urge to show off their wealth. A desire to appear frugal and modest, while secretly exuding personal success.

'This is an opportunity,' he said, his voice tight with urgency. 'A rare one. You won't find a company like this again.'

I asked about what venture and soon found out he had invested all his money in a ship that had sailed for Indonesia to buy spices. After the ship had left, he realized he had taken on too much risk and was now trying to find people to reduce his exposure. The rewards were high, but the losses could be ruining. The ship in which he held shares departed two months prior, and, not uncommonly, no one had heard from it since. Storms, pirates, tropical diseases, and the unknown threatened voyages between Amsterdam and the spice markets of Indonesia.

'I just need someone else to believe in this,' he said, softer now, the words nearly a plea.

He encouraged me to consider his offer, or beseech my husband or father to consider, assuming I could not make such decisions. I feigned girlish ignorance. Dutch society, even then, allowed women more control over their family. Women could engage actively in commerce, trade, and small-scale entrepreneurship. Many operated shops, taverns, bakeries, breweries, or took part indirectly through family businesses. Widows, especially, could inherit businesses and continue them independently. While not equal to men, Dutch law allowed women certain economic rights and the possibility of financial independence, particularly widows and unmarried women. This contrasted with the rest of Europe, where a woman's life was more constrained.

Another man came to me and politely hustled his insurance policies. I must have attracted attention. A new face in town, wearing relatively elegant clothes, was a potential mark. My accent did not raise suspicion. They all seemed to be from somewhere else. An ostrich plume in a large felt hat. A walking stick delicately engraved from Asia.

'So please tell me how this works,' I said. 'I buy a share in a ship that goes to Indonesia, and I get that share in the profits when it comes back?'

'We used to get a share of the cargo, but what am I going to do with twenty barrels of nutmeg?' said one trader. 'Now we can handle in cash, so much more convenient'.

'Yes, a market order is possible,' said a portly gentleman with a walking stick. A gold fob watch chain hung from his vest pocket. Not too much on display, but enough to announce its value. 'But there are other ways of making money'

A small crowd gathered, each wearing a perfume that helped drown out the stench from the nearby Rokin canal but created its own mélange of noxious aromas. Another gentleman chimed in. He was obviously not as rich as the portly gentleman. He had more worn and drab clothing, and there were some food stains on his laced collar.

'You could put a limit on the stock, so it sells at a specific price. A Stop order would do this automatically for you.'

'You could have a trailing stop order that moves with the stock price.' said another gentleman. He had a long dark overcoat lined with silk and fur.

Each gentleman seemed to have adorned his clothes with subtle flair, accessories from abroad, showcasing their specialties and experience with foreign things.

'I prefer Put Options' said another, and there was a groan from some of the group.

'Call me a fool...'

'You're a fool', said someone at the back

'...but Put Options are the way to go. Buy the right but not the obligation to sell at a certain price.'

'There are some who are Short Selling', said the portly gentleman. 'And even Naked Shorts, but ever since the Le Maire debacle, the VOC is very intolerant of such practices'. The crowd grumbled agreement.

'Or you could try Dark Pool Trading, but that depends on how much money you can invest in large blocks of stocks to avoid market impact'. The crowd laughed.

'Thank you, gentlemen for your generous education,' I said. 'I shall instruct my husband with your learnings'. The men bowed, and each gave me a scented card with their handwritten names and the address of a cafe where they frequently met. The maturity and sophistication of the share market surprised me, even though the world's first stock exchange had only just been established. Some things never change when it comes to money.

I walked across the bridge and onto the Zeedijk, a historic Amsterdam street now lined with cafes and businesses.

There was hustle and bustle, the same as in modern Amsterdam, but now, instead of tourists, these were local people selling their wares and services. A small, unwashed boy came up to me and tried to hand me a flyer, but I ignored him. He followed me, trying to push the paper into my hand.

'You have to take it!' he shouted. 'Otherwise I won't get paid!'

I accepted the paper. It was a flyer promoting a meeting at a cafe with a discussion with the philosopher Rene Descartes. The flyer listed today's date, April 24th, 1639, at 2:00 pm, and the Cafe Gerritsen on the Martelaarsgracht as the meeting place.

"*Theatrium Anatomicum* - 11:00pm" was written on the back. The boy whistled at someone and then ran off. I looked to see who he had whistled at, but only saw among the bustle a hooded, cloaked figure in the distance. But it could have been anybody.

The words "*Theatrium Antomicum*" were familiar. It reminded me of the painting that Rembrandt had made of the anatomical dissection by Dr. Tulp. I knew Rembrandt had painted it in De Waag. It seemed still early, so I walked down the Zeedijk to the Nieuwe Markt. There was De Waag, an impressive castle of a building on a Plein. There was a market going on, as farmers sold their vegetables and kept livestock in cages, ready for the kill.

Each corner of De Waag had a tower, each with its own entrance. I walked around it, looking at each entrance. Above each entrance was an inscription denoting the purpose of the rooms the door led to. "St. Lucas Gild" was above one, images depicting craftsmen was above another. The third, by the main entrance, had the image of a bearded man, and the words "*Theatrium Antomicum*". The door was locked.

'You don't want to go in there,' an old toothless man said. 'They cut up people in there. Not a sight for a pretty lady like you. It's an abomination if you ask me'. I smiled daintily, then walked on.

I knew where the Martelaarsgracht was, so I walked back towards the harbor where it was located. It was a beautiful day, and despite the smells from the canals and the rubbish in the streets, Amsterdam was looking young and glorious as she was growing into the city I loved.

The Cafe Gerritsen is a classic Amsterdam Brown Cafe, with a warm interior, dark wooden paneling, aged furniture, and low, ambient lighting. Although a relatively new cafe, nicotine had already stained the walls and ceilings and given a layer of grime to the glass windows. It was relatively bare inside, with worn furniture and kegs of beer. Against one wall were some Delft Blue tiles depicting a country scene.

In one corner, there was a group of people having a conversation that was lead by one man, a Frenchman, with a goatee and long black hair. He was holding court, and I realized it was the philosopher Rene Descartes.

'My dear friends, I bid you to begin your inquiries with doubt, for it is only by doubting that we may strip away all that is uncertain and arrive at that which is indubitable. Doubt everything. I resolved to discard all preconceived opinions and to examine each bias anew, as though I were building knowledge from the foundation up. I carved away at the fat of presumptions and in doing so, I discovered one truth that could not be doubted'.

He paused for dramatic effect. 'Do you know what that is?'

His audience, some slightly drunk, encouraged him. 'Go on, Rene.'

'That I think, and therefore, I exist—Cogito, ergo sum. This first certainty serves as the cornerstone upon which all further knowledge must be established, for if we are to seek truth, we must ensure that our foundation is unshakable.'

'I think, therefore I am', he concluded.

'I drink, therefore I am', said a wit at the back, from another table.

'I drink, therefore I can't' said the plump barkeeper. There was laughter from the crowd, and Descartes raised his glass in good humor and took a gulp. They all cheered.

'Therefore, let us embrace reason as our instrument, that we think, doubt as our starting point, and clarity as our goal, for only through methodical inquiry can we ascend from uncertainty to the light of true understanding.'

The young man sitting at Descartes's table seemed unimpressed. His accent was Dutch, but his clothes suggested his family came from abroad.

'So prey tell me Sir, do you think we have free will. That God gave us free will to think independently of him?'

'I do indeed, Sir, and you are?' asked Descartes.

'Baruch Spinoza, Sir, and an admirer of your work. However, I have my own thoughts on free will. Let us cast aside the notion that God is some distant, personal ruler who governs the world as a king might govern his subjects. Instead, I propose to you that God and Nature are one and the same—*Deus sive Natura*. Everything that exists, from the stars above to the ground beneath our feet, is God. There is no true randomness, no miracles that break the order of things—only the immutable laws of Nature, which we must strive to understand through reason.

There is no free will. And in this understanding, my friends, lies our freedom, for passions or fate does not enslave us, but we find peace in recognizing our place within this grand, eternal unity. Our actions, even the evil ones, are ultimately God's will, not ours'.

'So my friend,' said Descartes, 'as I raise this glass to my lips and drink this broth sold as wine, I do so not out of free will but because the laws of nature command me?'

'Exactly', said Spinoza.

'You may be right, why else would I drink this vinegar?' said Descartes. His audience laughed, and Spinoza took it in good humor.

I tried to remain unnoticed, as a lady in this kind of establishment was unusual. However, there was an older man over in the corner who had been staring at me. He then came over to me. He had a slight limp and the careful walk of an old man that did not want to fall. In his sixties, he was well-dressed, his long grey beard contrasting with surprisingly good teeth for a man of this period. Standing there for a few seconds, he just stared at me. I tried to avoid his gaze, and considered leaving.

'Is it really you?' he asked, finally. He looked almost upset.

'I don't know who you think I am,' I said.

'Is it you, Boudawijna!'

'How do you know me sir, have we met?'

'It's me. Vincent!'

Chapter 7

I could not believe it. It looked like a Vincent, or more accurately, Vincent's grandfather.

'I'm sorry, I don't understand', I said.

'It's me, Vincent. We used to hang out in Amsterdam, remember? It's been along time ago, at least for me. I've been here now for thirty years.' His thick, tousled hair was now thin and grey.

'Vincent? It's you?', I could not believe my eyes. 'How could this be, we were together only about six weeks ago?'

Vincent wrapped his arms around me and cried. It was him. I was in shock.

'After I left that evening I knew that we were in trouble. I was contacted a few days later and met with Lisbeth Van Os'.

'She's a piece of work', I said.

'They sent me back to Amsterdam, at the start of the VOC, the stock exchange. 1603. She said that I would have to stay here, and help the Guardians, or there would be consequences for the Dol clan. They sent me through the time vortex. I had to deal with problems with the setting up of the VOC. They would not let me back.'

'I can help you get back,' I said.

'It's too late, Bou. I have been here for thirty years, I'm an old man now, I wont go back to being a young man. I will still be old'.

'But you can go back all the same, be back with your family, your old life!'

'I have a life here now, Bou. I am married; I have 4 children. There were eight, but four have died. The healthcare here is primitive.'

'You, Vincent, have four children?'

'There is not much to do in the evenings. They have no WiFi.'

'Oh my god.' But then I was speechless.

'How did you get here how long have you been here?' he asked. I told him.

'You idiot'!' he said, and rubbed his face. 'And Lisbeth knows you are here?'

'Yes. I think she was the one who gave me this flyer to come here. Maybe she knew you would be here too'. He nodded. He had received a flyer as well. She meant us to meet.

'I'm not the man I used to be Bou. Thirty years have passed. I've had to do many things. It's a hard life in the seventeenth century. At first I was reluctant but when your second child has died you end up accepting the protection employment offers. It is my life. It is not bad. I read a lot, I play a musical instrument. I have an interest in philosophy, so it is interesting to see Descartes, and Spinoza, on their journey.'

I ordered a bottle of wine and some bread and cheese. Vincent wiped his eyes, but then smiled at me. 'I'm happy to see you again, Bou, I have thought about you a lot. The first few years here were very tough for me, but knowing you and the rest of the Dol tribe was safe helped me focus. It has not been a terrible life.' He then became quiet and more serious.

'There is something going on Bou,' he said. 'Look at that guy over there', and he nodded towards a finely dressed portly man sitting next to a window. On the table in front of him was a cushion with a tulip bulb on it.

'You won't believe the madness sweeping through the city, Bou! Just last week, a single tulip bulb—nothing more than a bit of earth and promise—sold for the price of a grand canal house. Merchants, bakers, even fishermen are abandoning their trades, all to gamble on these flowers. The Semper Augustus, that rarest of tulips, now fetches a fortune, and contracts for bulbs are traded like fine silks at the market. It's as if people have lost their senses, convinced that the value will never stop rising. But I tell you, this cannot last forever—what is a flower, after all, but a fleeting thing?'

'I see men who were once cautious in their dealings now mortgaging their homes just to purchase bulbs they will never even touch or plant. Speculation runs wild; men buy and sell futures on tulips they have never seen, only to resell them for double the price within days. At taverns and exchanges, the talk is of nothing but tulips, and fortunes are made and lost in an instant. My wife's cousin Willem, a humble carpenter, made more in a month than he ever did in a year.'

Vincent lowered his voice. 'I have been told by Lisbeth that her step-brother Frederik has been influencing the market to his own advantage. He is trying to drive up the prices and giving easy loans to merchants whom he is trying to ensnare when the market collapses.'

'Isn't that what they do, the guardians?' I asked.

'You see, the trick isn't just knowing what will happen—it's making sure it still happens the way it's supposed to,' Vincent said, lowering his voice as he swirled the wine in his glass. 'The guardians don't just travel back in time to make a profit; they must ensure history remains intact while doing it. They call themselves *The Syndicate*, and they operate under strict rules: no major disruptions, no personal attachments, and no greed beyond what history allows. A misplaced word, an ill-timed death, and suddenly the ripples become waves. That's where we 'servants' come in—loyal shadows, trained to nudge events back on course, to fix what wavers. If a deal goes too well, we introduce a balancing loss elsewhere. If a key figure falls ill too soon, we see to it he recovers just in time. Balance, Bou, is everything.'

Vincent leaned in; his eyes gleaming in the candlelight. 'Think about it: They knew when the South Sea Bubble would burst, but they made their fortunes before the crash. They are investing in the Dutch tulip trade, but never enough to be noticed. Gold, stocks, land—They move in and out of history like ghosts, taking only what won't be missed. The world never suspects, because to the world, they never existed. And if anyone strays? If a Syndicate member decides to alter fate for their own gain?' He smiled, but there was no warmth in it. 'Well... the servants handle that, too.'

'You mean Frederik?' I asked.

'Yes, he has gone rouge, made unsanctioned investments and lent cheap money to important strategic investors. He is trying to bankrupt them and take over their shares. These investors, and their descendants are needed in the future. But Fredrick wants all the power, he wants to control the syndicate.'

'And Lisbeth wants to control him?'

'Lisbeth loathes her step-brother, but she is powerless to stop him. Guardians cannot hurt Guardians, it's an ancient code.'

'So, you have to stop him?' I said. Vincent laughed. 'They are far too strong for me, and relatively indestructible. Also, the punishment for a servant who harms a Guardian, well, you don't want to know.'

'So Frederick is going rogue, and you are going to try and "handle" him?'

Vincent shrugged and took a sip of his wine. 'Lisbeth told me to sabotage the Tulip mania before it gets too far, before Frederik sucks too many important investors into bankruptcy. But he can't find out. Lisbeth has been doing damage control on him. She's been doing it for a while.'

The portly man stood up, and lifting the cushion from the table, walked out of the cafe. We watched him as he strutted to the door, holding up the cushion for everyone to see, but in a way that made it look like he didn't think it important.

'What an idiot', I said. 'The riches the merchants have are getting to their egos, but their Calvinist upbringing is conflicting with that. They have the human urge to brag but the social pressure to be modest. Maybe this is just an expression of that.'

'Wait, I have an idea, let's follow him,' said Vincent. 'Why?', I asked. But Vincent just grabbed me and pulled me towards the door. 'I'll explain, but we have to catch up, and I can't walk as fast as I used to'.

The portly man had not got very far, so we kept him in sight.

'He might go to another auction. They are usually private affairs with only people with wealth, or at least the money to spend. I've been following these idiots around for awhile.'

We went outside. The portly man had stopped at the cafe door and then put the tulip in his pocket. He nodded towards a burly tattooed man, who was leaning against a wall smoking a pipe. The man nodded back and escorted the portly man up the street. He was his bodyguard, a wise decision in what was still a lawless city.

They walked among the crowd up towards the Dam square, but poor Vincent could not keep up. He waved to me to keep going.

'I'll text you!' I said, but of course, that made no sense. The two men walked briskly for a while. The people in the street went around them as they ploughed their way to the city center. Eventually, the portly man stopped at another cafe. He pulled out the tulip bulb, placing it delicately back onto the cushion. The bodyguard leant against the wall, pulling out his pipe. They had not noticed me.

A hush of low conversation and the flicker of candlelight filled the wooden interior of the cafe. Heavy oak beams crossed the ceiling, and the scent of pipe smoke and spilled ale hung in the warm air. In one corner, a group of four sat around a rough-hewn table. The late autumn evening pressed its chill against the leaded glass windows, but inside, merriment and optimism radiated as brightly as the hearth in the corner. A half-burned tallow candle illuminated scattered papers on the table—papers scrawled with numbers, tulip names, and transactions that had taken place earlier that day. A few bulbs lay on the table.

At the head of the table sat a merchant they called Jan, a ruddy-cheeked man in a merchant's vest, enthusiastically gesturing with a quill pen. Beside him, Dirk, a younger craftsman-turned-trader, leaned forward eagerly, his sleeves rolled up as if ready to wrestle fortune itself. Pieter, older and more reserved, sipped spiced wine, but his eyes gleamed with the same fever as the others. And next to Pieter sat Petronella, who I took as an educated merchant's wife, her lace collar neat above a dark woolen dress. Though she offered a polite smile, her fingers tapped lightly on the rim of her cup, betraying a thoughtful unease.

In their midst, I felt both conspicuous and invisible—a young woman from a far-off future, trapped in this time. I approached the table, introduced myself, and commented on the wonderful ink drawings of tulip bulbs that lay on the table. I listened intently as the men began to excitedly explain their investments in the exotic flower bulbs that had seized Holland's imagination. They may be merchants, but they were definitely sales people.

Jan spread out one of the papers on the table, smoothing it with pride. On it were columns of florid script: names like *"Admiral van der Eijck," "Viceroy,"* and *"Semper Augustus,"* alongside sums of guilders so large that I nearly gasped. Jan's eyes shone in the candlelight as he tapped a line on the page.

'Just this morning,' he exclaimed, "a single bulb of *Viceroy* sold for *3,000 guilders!*" His voice was loud enough to turn a few heads from nearby tables. Lowering it slightly, he continued, "Can you imagine? Three thousand! Enough to buy a small townhouse by the canal." He chuckled, stroking his short beard. "And mark my words, by spring it shall be double that."

Dirk chimed in, 'I have two bulbs of *General van Eyck*,' he announced to me and Petronella with barely contained glee. 'Bought them for 400 guilders apiece last month, and today each is worth 1200. If I wait till next month...' He spread his hands as if the outcome was obvious—riches, growth, limitless increase. It seemed to me he was trying to convince Petronella, who looked anxious and unsure. She might have been on the cusp of investing, and the gentlemen were eager for her to do so.

I offered a polite smile. 'That is astonishing,' I said. 'I... I had no idea a flower could command such a price.'

'It's not just a flower, dear,' laughed Pieter, the older man. He had the dignified air of a long-time trader, perhaps a former spice merchant now bitten by the tulip bug. 'It is an investment, as solid as any venture with the East India Company.' Pieter drained the last of his wine and leaned forward, warming to his lecture. 'You see, the entire nation is in love with tulips. Everyone from wealthy burgers to humble cobblers is trying to get a bulb or two. The demand is ever-rising.' He pointed his pipe for emphasis, a curl of smoke wreathing his face. 'Simple economics: when demand is high and supply is low, prices rise. And supply—ah!' He wagged the pipe. 'These rare bulbs are not so easily multiplied. Some of the finest are prone to breaking – the virus that makes those beautiful flame-like streaks – and gardeners cannot just grow dozens overnight. The rarity remains.'

Jan slapped the table cheerfully. 'My friends, what Pieter says is true. We are on the brink of fortune such as Holland has never seen!' He looked around the table, catching Petronella's eye. 'Why, even my cousin sold his brewery to invest the money entirely in bulbs. He calls it tulip fever, and says it's the best thing that ever happened to him.'

Petronella managed a gracious nod. 'So I've heard,' she said. Her voice was measured, polite, but I noticed she did not share the men's laughter. 'My husband may purchase a few bulbs as well.' She paused, lifting the candle to better see the list in Jan's hand. 'The figures are impressive... truly.' Yet her dark eyes flicked to me, as if seeking an outside perspective amid this chorus of optimism.

I took a sip of small beer to gather my thoughts. It was surreal to witness this legendary speculation first-hand. I remembered reading about Tulip Mania in history books—how fortunes were made and lost in a blink, how a rare tulip could cost more than a house. Now here I sat, surrounded by people living it, blinded by their excitement. My heart pounded with the urge to cry out a warning. But how could I do so without revealing myself or sounding utterly mad? I set down my cup carefully, deciding to proceed with cautious reasoning masked as innocent questions.

I leaned forward, adopting a curious tone. 'Forgive me if this is a silly question,' I began, my fingers tracing the rim of her mug. 'I am new to Amsterdam's trade... What ensures that these prices will keep rising? Do people truly have so much money for tulips even now?"

Dirk was quick to reply, grinning. "Good question, not silly at all, juffrouw! You see, everyone expects the price to rise because it has been rising. If you don't buy now, someone else will, and you'll lose the chance at profit. So more and more people hurry to purchase, and that drives prices higher still." He spoke as though explaining to a child that summer follows spring.

Jan nodded vigorously. "Indeed. Last month I thought perhaps the prices were high, but look—this month they are higher yet. There is no end in sight!" He tapped his quill on the table for emphasis. "Every week, new folks enter the trade. Even my baker is trading bulbs in his spare time, and making more money than from bread. How could the prices possibly fall when everyone desires these flowers?"

I pressed gently, 'But... can everyone profit? For someone to buy, another must sell, ja?' I looked around the table innocently. 'What if, one day, many people wanted to sell at the same time? Who would be left to buy?'

The three men exchanged glances. Pieter shrugged off the question first. 'That day will not come anytime soon, my dear. Why would we all sell when the profits are growing by the day? Only a fool would get out of the tulip trade now.'

He gave a reassuring smile to Petronella, as if to include her in the circle of savvy investors. 'We florists—what they call us bulb traders—we have a saying: Today's price is high; tomorrow's will be higher.' He chuckled. 'Perhaps one day, years from now, the prices will level off, but by then we'll all be wealthy and content.'

Dirk took a long draught of his beer and added, 'I daresay, even if some did sell, there are so many newcomers waiting to snatch up bulbs. Why, just this evening, the tavern across the street is holding an auction. I heard people were clawing to bid on even common red tulips.' He shook his head in amusement. 'Common Rosa bulbs, can you imagine? Those used to be worth a guilder or two at most. Now even the simplest tulip fetches fifty!'

Jan reached for the wine bottle and refilled Petronella's cup, unasked, clearly confident that a celebration was soon to be in order. 'The appetite for tulips is endless. They've become a status symbol. Mynheer Van Loon down the road just planted a complete bed of them to show off his wealth. And others, not so rich, see that and dream of getting a bulb that might change their own fortunes.' He handed the cup back to Petronella, who accepted it with a faint smile. "You see, Miss Anne, tulips are now the lifeblood of the market. As safe as houses—no, safer! Houses can burn or flood, but a tulip bulb safely in the ground only multiplies.'

I felt a slight chill despite the warm room. Safer than houses... The phrase echoed ominously in my mind, knowing that some were literally trading houses for bulbs. She glanced at Petronella. The merchant's wife was listening intently, her gaze now lowered into the wine as if pondering Jan's words. I decided to try another tack.

'It is remarkable,' I said. 'In my homeland, I once heard a cautionary tale of a merchant who went bankrupt over a spice that suddenly fell out of fashion... But tulips, as you say, are different. They are beautiful indeed. Perhaps the demand will last forever.' My subtle hint hung in the air: nothing lasts forever.

Pieter chuckled in a patronizing way. 'Spices and other goods can be replaced or oversupplied, true. But tulips—ah, they enchant the eye and heart. If people love beauty, there will be demand. And fashion, my dear, is exactly what benefits us. Tulips are the newest fashion. No one wants to be left behind.' He set down his pipe and leaned back. 'If I may ask, what trade was your family in, Miss Boudewijna? You speak of merchants and fashion—perhaps textiles?'

I hesitated. I had to be careful about questions about myself in this era. 'Textiles, yes,' she lied softly. 'My father traded fine linens. I learned a bit about markets from him.' This seemed to satisfy Pieter, who smiled and nodded.

Before the men could launch into another boast, a server passed by with a tray. Jan caught his arm merrily. 'A round of your best Rhine wine for my friends here!' he declared, clearly in a generous mood. 'On me.' The servant nodded and moved off.

Jan turned back to the table and lowered his voice conspiratorially, though still loud enough for all to hear. 'You know,' he said, 'just between us, I heard that one *Semper Augustus* bulb traded last week for twelve acres of land outside Haarlem.' His eyes sparkled. 'Twelve acres! For a single bulb! Imagine the leverage we have in our hands with even a few of these.'

Dirk whistled appreciatively (though I suspected he had heard the story already). 'If only I could get my hands on a Semper Augustus... But even if I sold everything I own, I could not afford one.'

Jan waved that off. 'No matter, friend. There are plenty of other fine breeds. The trick is to buy low and sell high, step by step.' He puffed up with pride. 'Why, I started with just a handful of common bulbs last year. Traded up and up. Now I deal in rare ones like *Generals* and *Admirals*. Soon, I'll afford a Semper Augustus of my own.'

Petronella finally interjected with a gentle question. 'Jan, did you not tell me earlier you mortgaged your warehouse to raise funds for those last purchases?' Her tone was calm, but the question landed heavily for a moment.

Jan cleared his throat, a touch of color rising in his cheeks. 'A temporary measure, mevrouw, nothing more,' he said hastily. 'I used the warehouse as collateral, yes, but with the profits from the next sale, I shall pay off that note and then buy two more warehouses!' He laughed, a bit too sharply. 'It's like—like planting one bulb to get ten. You'll see.'

I noticed Petronella's fingers tightening around the stem of her wine cup. The merchant's wife lowered her eyes. 'I see,' she replied quietly.

The wine arrived, and Jan eagerly poured for everyone, determined to keep the mood celebratory. Glasses were raised and clinked. 'To fortune made from flowers!' Dirk toasted. 'To the prosperity of Holland!' added Pieter. They all drank, savoring the sweet German wine.

I sipped mine only lightly. She could feel tension beneath the joviality now. Petronella had hardly touched her previous drink, and the new wine in her cup trembled slightly in her hand. I decided to ask one last question—one that might plant a seed of caution without revealing too much.

She set down her glass and spoke into a lull in the conversation. 'These contracts you trade... they are for bulbs to be delivered in the future, ja?'

Dirk nodded. 'In the spring, when the bulbs can be dug up after they bloom. Until then, we trade paper guarantees. But worry not—come spring, each bulb will be worth even more than now. We just trade the promise of them, to save time.'

'It sounds clever' I said, 'but I wonder... what if when spring comes, those who promised to buy find they cannot pay the agreed price?'

Jan let out a mocking laugh. 'Cannot pay? Who would dare enter a contract they cannot fulfill? In this business, a man's word and money are at stake. If anyone tried to cheat, their name would be shamed in all the guilds.' He wagged a finger. 'Besides, by spring, many will have sold their contract to another for profit. In truth, some buyers never intend to plant the bulb at all—only to trade the contract onward. It's all in good faith down the line.'

Pieter added with an amused grin, 'They call it the wind trade, these futures, because nothing changes hands at the moment but air and promises. Yet, as Jan says, everyone believes the promise is as good as gold.' He gave a slight shrug. "Perhaps it seems strange to you, but it's the modern way of trade."

I managed a faint smile. 'Yes... I suppose it is.' In my time, I had seen modern stock markets and derivatives; the chaotic scene of 1630s tulip contracts was both familiar and frightening in its naivety. I could almost feel the fragile bubble expanding around them, shimmering with beautiful colors like a soap bubble... ready to burst.

'It does seem like a bubble to me' I said.

'A bubble?' said Jan. They all looked at each other and repeated the word, looking for clarity, each with his own accent and inflexion.

'Bubble?'

'Bubble?'

'Bubble'?'

'What do you mean, a bubble?'

I glanced at Petronella, who had fallen silent. The older woman stared at the golden wine in her cup as if it were a scrying glass. Finally, Petronella spoke up, her voice quieter than before.

'A bubble is something that can burst', she said. 'Gentlemen, might there not be wisdom in realizing some of these gains? Perhaps selling one or two bulbs now to secure a bit of profit? After all, one never knows when fate might turn.' She attempted a light laugh. 'Even a sudden frost can spoil a tulip crop... or a ship from the Levant might arrive with some new novelty that captures everyone's fancy instead.'

Jan and Dirk exchanged looks of mild surprise—hearing such caution from the usually quiet Petronella was unexpected. Dirk patted her arm kindly. 'Ah, mevrouw, you sound like my mother. She too worries I should 'cash out,' as she calls it, after I tripled her dowry on bulbs.' He chuckled. 'But if I sell now, I miss the even greater profits coming next. Why take a little profit when you could soon have a fortune? As for fate turning—fate favors the bold!'

Jan drained his wine and set the glass down firmly. 'Aye. I have waited my whole life for an opportunity like this. The gods of trade smile on us.' His words were confident, but for the first time I detected a note of defiance in them, as if he were pushing away an unwelcome thought. 'I'll not snatch at pennies and lose out on pounds.' He attempted a reassuring smile at Petronella.

Petronella pressed her lips together and gave a slow nod. 'Of course. I only meant... one should be prudent.'

There was a small, momentary silence. The crackle of the hearth filled it, along with distant laughter from another table where a few drunken sailors sang a shanty. My heart went out to Petronella; I could sense the older woman's inner conflict. Something about this wild tulip game unsettled her sensible nature.

I decided the best I could do was support Petronella's cautious instinct without rousing the men's ire. I spoke gently, 'Prudence is never unwise, sirs. Even the most splendid summer has the occasional storm. But I understand—your confidence comes from success you've seen with your own eyes.' I offered a conciliatory smile to Jan and Dirk. 'Perhaps you are right and these flowers will keep blooming fortunes for all forever.'

Relieved to steer back to positivity, Dirk raised his refilled cup. 'To blooming fortunes, indeed!' he exclaimed. Jan and Pieter echoed the toast, and the men drank once more. The brief shadow of doubt seemingly passed.

Petronella took a small sip as well, but her eyes met mine over the rim of her cup. In that glance, I saw gratitude and resolve: the merchant's wife had heard the subtle warning. Petronella offered me the slightest nod, as if to say she would remember this conversation. Perhaps later, she would speak with her husband, urge a bit of caution, or at least secure some profit before it was too late.

The men launched into another round of exuberant stories — Jan was now recounting how a bulb he sold had changed hands ten times in a single day, each buyer making a profit in hours. Dirk boasted a neighbor traded his entire dairy herd for a handful of tulips and was congratulating himself on the deal. Their laughter rang out, full of blind optimism, filling the cozy cafe with an infectious energy.

The men's laughter echoed loudly in the café, their certainty unwavering. I felt a surge of frustration rising in her chest. I loathed their patronizing attitude, especially as I knew I was right, but I could not tell them how. My carefully chosen words, my subtle warnings—they had all fallen on deaf ears. These men, blinded by their own confidence, refused to see reason. Petronella sat quietly, eyes lowered, her fingers nervously tracing patterns on the tablecloth. I had to convince them of the danger they were facing, but more importantly, break the mania before Frederick van Os could bankrupt too many people.

Finally, unable to hold my tongue any longer, I reached abruptly for one of the tulip bulbs Jan had left carelessly lying beside his papers. I held it up, drawing startled gazes from around the table.

'This?' I asked, holding the brown, papery bulb aloft. My voice trembled slightly with suppressed emotion. 'You trade fortunes, houses, and livelihoods for this?'

Before any of them could respond, I impulsively brought the bulb to my lips and took a firm bite. The dry outer layers cracked audibly beneath my teeth, a bitter, dusty taste flooding my mouth. It was disgusting, and I spat it out. I forced herself not to flinch, staring defiantly at the shocked faces of Jan, Dirk, and Pieter. Petronella's eyes widened in astonishment, a hand rising instinctively to her lips.

'This bulb—this thing you've mortgaged your homes for—is nothing' I declared firmly, setting the half-bitten bulb down on the table. 'No gold inside, no magic, no lasting value. Just a bitter, worthless root.'

A stunned silence fell over the table. Dirk blinked rapidly, his mouth hanging open. Jan flushed deeply, anger mixing with confusion. Pieter frowned, shaking his head in disbelief. Only Petronella watched me closely, her thoughtful expression gradually shifting into quiet understanding.

'You must forgive me,' I said, my anger ebbing. 'But ask yourselves honestly—when the madness fades, will this dry bulb feed your families or shelter your heads?'

Petronella reached forward cautiously and picked up the ruined bulb, examining it in the candlelight. Her gaze lifted slowly to the men around her. 'This woman speaks harshly, but perhaps rightly,' she said softly. 'What if we are chasing nothing more than bitter roots?'

The men exchanged uncomfortable glances, their earlier bravado now visibly shaken. I leaned back in my chair, heart still pounding but relieved that at last, perhaps, I had planted a seed of doubt strong enough to take root.

'That, my dear' said Jan, pointing at the half-bitten bulb, 'is an onion.' But somehow, I think my point had been made.

Just then Vincent arrived, out of breath. 'I think we should leave,' he said. Then he bowed to Petronella. 'Ma'am, nice to meet you, you are looking radiant'. Petronella smiled. We left quickly; Vincent seemed to be in a hurry.

When we got outside, he seemed flustered. 'What did you do in there?' he asked.

'I was just telling them about the dangers of investing in a bubble. They were very patronizing'

'That was Mevrouw Petronella, she is one of the wealthiest women in Amsterdam. Wealthier than all those other men at the table. If you have convinced her of avoiding the tulips, then that is one of the main investors we are trying to protect. But we must be subtle. We can't just eat the tulips.' He didn't seem happy. I agreed my tactic was not to be repeated.

'Come with me to my house, you need nourishment.' he said. I nodded. It was funny to hear him say words like 'nourishment'. He had been here too long.

His house was near the Jordan. An area to the side of the main canals that had smaller houses and lots of vegetable gardens. The house was one of the larger ones in a wealthier district. His wife was gracious, and his four children ran around me, excited by the unknown visitor. His wife prepared some food, and we drank some fortified wine.

'I was thinking,' I said. 'I can try and get back to the future and then get them to return you before you get settled. If we can stop this tulip mania in its tracks, and stop Frederick, maybe we can get into Lisbeth's good books'

Vincent smiled. 'Let me show you something,' and he called one of his children.

'Boudewijna, meet Boudewijn'. It was a child of about eight years. The boy smiled shyly, and struggled to get out of his father's arms, and then ran off.

'I know, that would be hard, missing your children.'

'It's not just that,' said Vincent. 'That child is Boudewijn Dol. He is your great great great whatever grandfather. If I go back before I start a family, you will not exist, because he will not. So you can see, I can never go back, and I have accepted that. It's not so bad here. The food is delicious, and there's so much more community. We all need each other. There's also no rush here. Things get done when they get done.'

'Vincent, I don't know what to say.' I said, and he held my hand. 'Let's drink some wine, and you must rest.' he said.

'So anything small happening here can have great consequences?', I said.

'Exactly.'

'We sat in silence for a while. We watched the children play, then watched his wife Catrina try to herd them all to bed. I knew that Vincent could never go back.

'It is an interesting place, seeing the start of modern western capitalism. It was such a privilege to see the likes of Descartes and Spinoza. This is Amsterdam in its glory time. I know Spinoza thinks we are all slaves to a determined fate, while Descartes thinks we have a will. But I think we are slaves to time, time and its consequences.' I said. Vincent nodded in agreement. We talked until the last of the candles had burnt down.

Vincent had a spare room, having chased his children into another. I was surprised by how little stuff cluttered the rooms. Mass production was still in the future. In the corner was a bedstee, so I climbed in. The cramped space didn't bother me; I was exhausted and welcomed the solitude to gather my thoughts. Vincent didn't know about the note on the back of the flyer, which read, "*Theatrium Anatomicum - 11:00pm*". I had to go to that, see who had sent me the flyer. I didn't want to alarm Vincent or get him further involved.

Later, according to the striking of the Westerkerk clock tower, it was now 10:30 pm. When I thought everyone was asleep, I quietly slipped out from the bedstee and made my way out into the street.

Chapter 8

The night air in Amsterdam was crisp and biting as I stepped onto the cobblestone streets. Lanterns hung sparsely along my path, casting pools of flickering orange light on the old bricks and shuttered windows, leaving stretches of shadowy uncertainty in between.

I quickened my pace, pulling my woolen cloak tighter around my shoulders. My destination was De Waag, the imposing stone weigh house looming at the center of Nieuwmarkt Square. Its silhouette stood black and stark against the faint glow of moonlight.

A noise startled me, causing me to spin around sharply. Only a stray cat skittered across the street, its eyes glinting briefly before it disappeared into shadows. I steadied my breath, silently reprimanding myself for nerves. I pressed on, the click of my shoes echoing softly as I neared De Waag.

When I finally reached the vast square, I paused, scanning the shadows. There were people about, some drunk, others talking, arguing. They were at the cafes to the west of De Waag. De Waag itself was silent. All its doors were locked. I went to the door in one turret with the words "*Theatrum Anatomicum.*" above it.

I tried the heavy wooden door, finding it unlocked. With a deep breath, I slipped inside and ascended the dark narrow spiral staircase, the stone walls pressing in closely around me. My footsteps echoed softly, each step pulling me maybe closer to answers—or perhaps greater danger.

At the top of the stairs, I stepped cautiously into a room dimly illuminated by moonlight. The air thick with dust and the sour bite of old tallow. My eyes widened in horror and fascination. On a central table lay the disassembled body of a criminal recently hanged, his skin pale and lifeless in the flickering glow. His left arm was openly dissected, sinews exposed vividly, exactly as Rembrandt had painted in "*The Anatomy Lesson of Dr. Nicolaes Tulp.*" The top of his skull had been opened, and his brain exposed. Silence pressed heavily upon me, disturbed only by the faint hiss of candle flame. The flickering of the candle gave the illusion that the body was moving. Was he breathing? I swore I could see his fingers moving. His brain pulse.

'Remarkable, isn't it? The human body, the primitive way they explore it' said a quiet voice from the shadows.

I spun around, heart pounding. A tall, shadowy figure stood at the far end of the room. He had been observing me.

In the dark, I could not see who it was. 'I got your flyer. Obviously,' I said, steadying my trembling voice. I wanted to check to see if it indeed was he who sent the flyer.

He stepped forward slightly, his features still hidden. 'Why are you here in this time period? Who sent you'.

I hesitated, glancing once more at the dissected body on the table before summoning my resolve. Even though I could not see his face, I knew it was Fredrick van Os.

'Was it Lisbeth?' he asked.

'I travelled here on my initiative. I was seeking my cousin Vincent, and I found him. That's all I want' I said.

He started towards me, and I moved away. We circled the table; the corpse seemed to watch our movements.

'I know nothing of her, or what she wants,' I said. 'I have found Vincent in good health, I am satisfied, and now I wish to return.'

'You have nothing to wish, you are a mere servant.'

'I do not consider myself to be such, but Vincent certainly is a dedicated servant who has served the Guardians well.' I said.

'Then why has he been trying to sabotage' - and here he sought the right word '- my initiative?'

I felt that to run from him was to show weakness, and I knew I could not escape, so I stood my ground. 'You mean the tulip mania - that was always doomed to failure. We know this.'

'Of course, but on my terms.' he said. The light from the moon now shone on his face. It was indeed Fredrick, and he had hatred in his eyes. My back hit the cold plaster wall. Nowhere left to go.

He was on me in a flash. A hand around my throat, cold and dry like old wood. The other pressed my shoulder to the wall. I fought, kicked, twisted—but it was like struggling against stone.

'Don't,' I rasped. 'Please.'

He said nothing. His face came close—too close—and I felt the sharp flash of pain as his teeth sank into my neck. My body seized. A gasp stuck in my throat.

But then—he jerked. A strangled, wet hiss left his throat. He pulled back suddenly, shaking. Smoke curled from his lips, his face, his hands. His eyes, once gleaming with hunger, were wide now. Furious. Confused.

He looked down.

The necklace—ultramarine beads, strung close to my skin—lay between them, stained with blood. Where it had touched him, his flesh sizzled.

My knees buckled. I slumped to the floor, clutching my neck. My head spun, blood pulsing thick in my ears. I could feel the venom working already—something cold moving through me.

Fredrick staggered a few steps back, swiping at his face, snarling. Then he turned back toward me.

I fumbled in my pocket. My fingers closed around the tangled mass of rosaries and the cheap beaded necklaces I had taken.

He lunged.

I screamed and thrust both hands forward, ramming the fistful of beads into his gapping fanged mouth.

He choked. He clawed at my arms. Then screamed—loud and inhuman—as the beads seared the inside of his mouth and throat, leaving him paralyzed. Smoke poured from his jaw, his eyes bulging. He flayed at his mouth, but his muscles had seized, his control lost.

He tried to pull away, but I grabbed the back of his head and held him there, teeth clenched, every muscle shaking.

The vampire writhed, limbs thrashing, body convulsing. His skin blistered, cracked. He tore free—but too late. His body was already breaking down.

He collapsed, his form unraveling into a dessicated mummy, smoking on the floor.

I collapsed against the wall, blood soaking my collar, chest heaving. The beads lay scattered around me, glowing faintly in the moonlight seeping through the shutters.

I touched my neck. The wound was already closing. But the cold in my veins remained. Something inside me had already begun to change.

The silence in the room was suffocating. Ash clung to the floorboards where the vampire had died, and the smell of scorched flesh lingered. I sat motionless, my back against the wall, staring at the scattered beads.

My hands were shaking. Not from fear—at least, not entirely.

I wiped my neck. My fingers came away slick and red. But the wound had already closed. I could feel it: a tight, foreign sensation under the skin, as if my body was stitching itself together from the inside out.

My heart still beat, but slower. Too slow. I pressed a hand to my chest. The rhythm was there, but faint. Detached. Like a memory.

My mouth was dry. Not the usual thirst. This was deeper. Sharper. My throat burned. The taste of metal flooded my mouth—copper, thick and warm.

Blood.

My skin looked pale under the moonlight, but it wasn't just the blood loss. It was something else. Something permanent. I tried to move, gasping, but immediately felt my strength fading. My vision blurred, my head spinning. The bite marks pulsed at my neck, spreading a cold, deadly energy through my veins. The lapis lazuli necklaces felt like acid, weighing more than I could ever move, and I understood with dreaded clarity what was happening.

The vampire's bite had begun to change me—yet the ultramarine poison now burning my skin and coursing through my blood was killing me. As darkness overtook my vision, I lay trapped on the cold stone floor, trapped helplessly between death and eternal life. Pinned to the cold floor by ultramarine stones that weighed nearly nothing. What had killed him was now killing me.

My vision blurred, but I could see another figure. It was a woman.

Disgusted, she kicked the corpse of Frederick out of the way. She then went to the dead corpse of the dissected criminal on the table and snaps of his arm like a twig. Manipulating the sinews in his arm, the woman gets the dead arms' fingers to move, picking off the necklaces from my body. She then slides one of the dead fingers under the necklace on my neck, across my skin, pulling the finger closed and then ripping the necklace off, flinging it across the room. She drops the arm with disgust and wipes her hands with a handkerchief.

Breath came back into my lungs. The spasms subsided. She just stood there watching me. I drifted off into unconsciousness, but then she kicked me in the side.

'Ouw!'

She rolled her eyes. 'So, you are not dead then', she said, obviously disappointed. 'Not yet,' I said.

She leans over me, lifting one eyelid to look and my pupils, then she sticks her fingers in my mouth feeling my teeth. My mouth felt parched, and my gums were numb. Her fingers tasted of leather.

'Stop that!', I spluttered. She prodded me some more, and I felt a dark rage - 'STOP THAT!' I said again, but this time my mouth felt as if I had huge teeth, and it gave my speech a strange whistle. I tasted blood in my mouth, I had bit my tongue.

'Well, I can't say I'm not displeased that my horror of a step-brother is gone', she said, looking at the desiccated steaming body lying on the floor. Then she put her face close to mine, staring at me with a hatred and a meanness that had been her life for centuries - 'But does that mean I have simply exchanged one problem for another? My plan was to have him kill you, then have him put before the syndicate and reprimanded. That you have killed him, in self-defense, should have been a plus. But now that the idiot has turned you to one of us. Ugh.'

She stood up and looked at me with total distaste. 'God, why is *everything* a struggle?' she spat.

'Sorry about that', was all I could manage. 'I just want to keep my family safe.' I said, trying to stay conscious. Putting my hand to mouth, I felt the fangs. The sharpness pricked my finger. Now I really felt dizzy.

'You want to keep your family safe? I have been doing that for centuries - cleaning up this fool's mistakes' she said - pointing at the corpse of Fredrick. Through her hatred and bitterness, I could see a faint smile crack her lips. She was finally free of him.

I heard someone enter the room. He was wheezing and had a limp. It was Vincent. 'Bou!' he said and knelt beside me. 'Are you okay?'

'I've been better', I said.

'What happened here?' here asked.

'She will tell you later.' said Lisbeth. She leaned over and grabbed Vincent by his collar. 'But listen carefully Vincent, she is one of my tribe now. So, you take care of her. And when she is ready, bring her to me. And clean this mess up.'

And with that, she was gone.

'Oh my god, Bou, what have you done?' said Vincent.

I did not know, and I passed into unconsciousness. I remember being in the back of a horse-drawn carriage, and then finally being helped into the bedstee at Vincent's house.

The next few days were one of rest and recuperation. Vincent was distraught that I had now been turned to being a Guardian. He warned me of what was now my life.

'You will be exponentially stronger, so be careful when dealing with mere mortals. You will not be affected by sunlight, but that will become an issue as you grow older. We have already seen the effects of ultramarine. I did not know that this was a weakness for them. I will keep your necklaces, they may one day come in handy.'

He admitted that me being a Guardian would give an extra layer of protection to him and the Dol family. 'But this is not what I wanted. I think it's too big a sacrifice!'

'I will be all right, Vincent,' I said. And quietly I knew I had gotten what I wanted, for the threats to the Dol family, to making Vincent disappear, to the abuse of my sister. I had gotten revenge. Fredrick Van Os was no more.

Finally, I had enough strength to take a walk around my beloved city. The air smelled of damp stone, river water, and something rich and yeasty—bread, maybe, or beer. The streets of Amsterdam in 1630 were alive in a way that made the modern world feel almost sterile. I moved carefully along the edge of a canal, where the houses loomed narrow and impossibly tall, their gables like the teeth of some great wooden beast.

The roads were slick with rain, the sky a stretch of shifting grays. Traders called out in Dutch, their vowels sharp, their laughter rolling over the water. A man in a broad-brimmed hat pushed past me, his coat brushing against my arm, and I caught the scent of tallow and pipe smoke. I watched him step onto a boat tied at the canal's edge, where barrels were being hoisted onto the deck, men moving with practiced ease.

Everything seemed smaller than I now remembered. The streets tighter, the bridges closer together, the shops packed in like puzzle pieces. I passed a market where women in coifs and aprons haggled over fish, their fingers quick as they inspected the catch. The smell of herring and salt filled my nose.

Further down, I paused in front of a print shop, mesmerized by the copperplate engravings displayed in the window. Maps of the world as it was known in 1630's, curling at the edges. The continents looked misshapen, their coastlines uncertain, and yet these pages held the power to shape men's ambitions, to send ships toward unknown lands. It was right that these men should explore, without the hinderance of others having insider knowledge, of unfair practices. Inside, a printer in ink-streaked sleeves was setting type, his hands moving with steady precision. I enjoyed watching his craftsmanship. He was lost in his art, not even noticing me observe him.

I pressed my fingers to the cool glass, wanting to tell him that in my time, the world had already been mapped, that the great unknowns had been named. But I also knew it would not matter. To him, the future was an unread page. And that was the beauty of this age, the wonders still to come.

Church bells rang in the distance, their echoes rolling through the streets. I let the city carry me forward again, deeper into a time that did not belong to me but, for now, had taken me in.

Entranced by the city, I walked for hours, and before I knew it, it was getting dark. Then, turning a corner, I found myself standing in front of the "House with the Blood Stains". Searching for the message that Vincent had left me and saw nothing. I realized he had not written the message.

The next night I returned with a sharp knife and in a bag with a small bead of Lapis Lazuli - ultramarine - and marked the soft sandstone just as I had seen them in the future. I held the small bead with a pair of tongs and scrapped ultramarine on the letters. I could feel my energy draining as I worked, the negative powers of the bead working on me.

The next day Vincent told me that Lisbeth wanted to see me at her house on the Herengracht.

'It is time for me to go back', I said to Vincent, and he nodded.

'Vincent, if you ever need me to return, send me a message. The front of my apartment is the original facade, it is from sandstone. Carve the letter B, and when I see that, I will know you will need my help'.

He smiled. 'I will be fine, my job is to take care of Boudewijn, and I will be protected because of that.'

We embraced, and unsure of what fate would have in store for both of us, I left.

I was let into the house, which was now sunlight, the curtains wide open. Apparently, darkness was not a problem for Lisbeth.

'How are you feeling?' she asked, forcing some sort of social etiquette, now that I was a member of her tribe.

'Better, still confused', I said. She served coffee and told me to listen. I was to keep quiet and behave and there would be no consequences. She informed me I would be introduced to the Syndicate and trained in their ways.

'Don't you get tired of threatening everyone around you?' I asked.

'I get tired of trying to stop everything falling apart', she said. And now she was tired of me. 'Come, it is time for you to leave,' she said and led me to the basement door. Down the stairs I could see the water, dark and ominous, swirling below. I turned to her. 'Are you sure I will be safe on the other side?' I asked.

'Yes', she said, and kicked me in the chest so I flew back like a thrown rag doll.

I fell into the water backwards, and I struggled. The blackness surrounded me, but when I looked up, I could see the bright moon above me. I felt indestructible, and just floated deep in the water, letting the absence of anything around me calm me. There was no rush; I could surface whenever I wanted. I am immortal.

Eventually, a hand reaches in and grabs me, pulling me into a dinghy. It was Hiro. I asked him how he knew I would be here and he told me a woman called Lisbeth had told him. I must have looked pale in the moonlight, a ghostly Guardian pale. I smiled to reassure him, but then forgot I might have fangs and put my hand over my mouth. He was silent as we made our way back to the banks of Manhattan. I had a lot of explaining to do. Whether or not that would be the truth, that would depend on how much danger it would bring to him.

In France, the scent of lavender drifts on the evening breeze, mingling with the damp earth and sun-warmed stone. My boots press into the gravel of the lane, each step crunching softly, steady now, deliberate. The dust of distant places still clings to my coat, my skin, my thoughts, but here—here, the world feels slower. Familiar. I had not told my family I was coming and had walked up from the station.

My parents' chateau rises ahead, its golden façade kissed by the last light of day. The shutters are open, as they always were, inviting in the air of the hills. The ivy on the east wall has crept higher, twisting in wild abandon. How long has it been? Not long, and yet forever.

I turn onto the driveway, and there, in the garden, I see Papa.

His back is to me at first, tending to the roses. Even from here, I can see the precision in his movements, the way he coaxes life from the stems with careful hands. He has not changed. And yet—when he turns, when his eyes meet mine—I see it. A flicker of something deep, something heavy.

He straightens. The shears slip from his fingers, landing in the grass with a quiet rustle.

For a moment, we simply stand there. The weight of absence, of all the things unspoken, presses between us. And then, without a word, he crosses the garden, his steps quickening, his face unreadable. My throat tightens as he stops before me, his gaze searching.

'You're home,' he murmurs. There's relief in his voice, yes, but also sorrow.

I nod, unable to speak past the lump in my throat.

His hands hover for a moment, uncertain, before he finally gathers me into his arms. I sink into his embrace, the warmth of him grounding me in a way I hadn't realized I needed. The rest of the family run out to the garden.

'Papa,' I whisper against his shoulder.

'You've been through so much,' he says, his voice rough. He pulls back just enough to study my face, his thumb grazing my cheek as if to reassure himself I am real.

I try to smile, but it falters. 'I'm here now.'

'Yes,' he says, his eyes glistening. 'You are.'

And in this moment, with the grasshoppers humming in the lavender fields and the chateau standing steadfast behind us, I finally believe it.

My family is safe. My revenge, sweet. I am their Guardian.

www.ingramcontent.com/pod-product-compliance
Lightning Source LLC
Chambersburg PA
CBHW020654180626
46816CB00003B/1281